THE MEASURE OF A MAN

BY

JERRI HINES

http://jerrihines.org/

Sign up for Jerri's News email:
http://madmimi.com/signups/257394/join

Published by Magnolia Way

Copyright 2020 by Jerri Hines
Cover Art by Erin Dameron-Hill
Edited by Michelle Babb
Second Edit by Penny Friday Baker, Baker Blooper Editing

ISBN 978-1-7357513-2-0

DEDICATION

In memory of Coach Gerald Caveness

The Measure of a Man

FOREWORD

In the fall of 1960, Gerald Caveness, my dad, started coaching basketball at New Site High School in New Site, Mississippi. After coaching at much larger schools, he took the job to be closer to family. New Site was situated in the middle of what was known as Basketball Country.

It was the beginning of an incredible story.

This remarkable story is the inspiration behind *The Measure of a Man*. In this fictional account of the Royals' incredible run, I wanted to convey the man Dad was and the importance of having a mentor in your life. I wanted readers to get a glimpse of the Mississippi, where I was raised. I wanted the impressive feat accomplished by a group of remarkable young men led by a phenomenal coach to be remembered.

I have talked to so many of Dad's ballplayers. Most of what you will read is based on those conversations.

Dad cared about every player he coached. More important than wins, he believed in his kids, teaching them more than basketball.

Having served in the Marines, Dad had a staunch work ethic with hard-nosed discipline. He also had an overwhelming, driving desire to succeed.

He always believed there was a way to win no matter the odds.

Behind the coach was a man, a dad. The man I knew wasn't much different than I imagine he was as a coach.

Dad was a workaholic and taught us by example. We used to pray he would get a summer job. If he didn't, we would be working all summer long. One summer, all four of us hoed out an entire cotton field. Dad said we needed to know what hard work really was.

There was more to Dad than a coach. He loved his family and home. He taught history and instilled in all his kids that love and respect for those that came before us, not to mention his uncanny ability to train dogs.

Dad taught us to judge a man by his actions, not by the way he looked. I believe we grew up in one of the most unbiased households in Mississippi.

Though in my eyes, he was perfect. In reality, I realize he was only human. Yet, he never let those human flaws define the man he was.

Dad wasn't a person one could ignore. He would elicit some emotional response from you when you met him, whether it was love or hate.

There was no middle ground with Dad.

Moreover, he made no apology for the man he was.

Time has moved on. Dad is no longer with us. His feats as a coach are now only a distant memory, but I felt a need to preserve the history of that moment when Coach Gerald Caveness helped boys become men.

I hope that this story will inspire someone to believe in themselves and do the impossible.

Mississippi High School Basketball

Mississippi began to have State champions in basketball in 1922. Through the years, the tournament grew to where the high school association began breaking up the schools into divisions based on attendance. For the 1964-65 season, Mississippi High School Association divided the schools into four divisions for the first time: AA, A, BB, and B. AA had the most students enrolled in their school; B had the least number of students.

Each division would have its State champion. The State Tournament for each division would begin at the end of the regular season. Every team would enter the District tournament. From there, the top two teams would advance to the North Half or South Half, depending on the school's location. There was a total of four Districts in both the North and South. At the North or South Half tournament, there would be eight teams vying for the top three positions to advance to their State Tournament. At the State Tournament, there would only be one winner.

With this division into four classifications, the Mississippi High School Association set up the ultimate tournament to crown the overall champion. This tournament was called the Grand Slam. The Grand Slam pitted each State champion against each other, with BB playing B and AA playing A. The winner of each of the games would face each other for the title of Grand Slam Champion.

Prentiss County is located in Northeast Mississippi. Back in the 1960's, this area was known as Basketball Country. The county lived for its basketball. The communities included Baldwyn (BB), Booneville (A) and county seat, Jumpertown (B), Marietta (B), New Site (B), Thrasher (BB), and Wheeler (B). Across the south country line sits Lee County, where Tupelo (AA) is situated.

BASKETBALL

Basketball is more than a game.

Basketball is hard work, endless hours of practice, driving yourself to your limit, never quitting, picking yourself up after a fall, and doing it all over again. It's knowing and executing your role to the best you can be.

More important is to work together with your teammates to accomplish your goal. Understand that you are only as good as your team.

When things don't go your way or you might feel life hasn't been fair to you, you never abandon your dreams. Not everyone goes down the same road to accomplish a goal. You might have to take another road to the end you hope to achieve.

But whatever course you choose, you never stop believing in yourself.

You don't necessarily have to *be* the best to achieve your dream; you only have to do your best. For when a team works in unison for a common goal, there is no limit to what that team can accomplish.

Basketball is much more than a game.

It is a way to live your life.

Coach Gerald Caveness
1932-1990

The Measure of a Man

Season 1964-65

Chapter One

"Doggone it, Troy!" Ducking under the barbed-wire fence, I stumbled running after my brother. "You ain't going without me."

With his hands on his hips, Troy turned and grimaced. "Dean, stay home. It's our last night to coon hunt before training starts."

"Nope." I shook my head. "I'll tell Momma. I swear, I will."

Troy stared at me with intense dark eyes. He knew I bluffed. I wouldn't do that to him, but I wanted to go so bad with Freddie and him. Momma would have our hides if she caught us going out at midnight. She expected us to be up for church bright and early. At the moment, though, she was dead asleep in the house, having worked six long shifts in a row.

"Go ahead and let him come." Freddie gestured with his hand. "We gotta go."

With a shrug, Troy relented. "Well, don't just stand there."

I didn't hesitate but broke into a run to catch up with my brother. Freddie had parked his old, rusted Chevy truck out close to the road. He didn't dare drive up to the house and wake Momma.

With flashlights in hand, Troy and I ran through Old Man Sander's cow pasture. Thankfully, the moon was full, and the sky was clear, which helped light my way because my flashlight wasn't that bright. Honestly, I was surprised it worked. I had found it out in the old shed behind our house.

Freddie waited by the truck. Dressed in a dark flannel shirt and jeans, he stood there with a fish-eating grin on his face.

He was about the same height as Troy, but he looked like he was taller, what with being so skinny, like he never ate or something. Funny thing, he never stopped eating. Even now I knew, he was hiding a Mars bar in his back pocket.

He wouldn't get to do that on Monday. Training for basketball season started then.

Coach Carver had a whole list of rules for the players: no candy or soda except for orange soda, ten o'clock curfew—nine on the night before a game— and haircuts had to be above the ears. Troy had told me that Coach expected his boys to be willing to sacrifice.

I wasn't so sure about that sacrifice. Everyone else around here thought Coach Joe Carver was a god or something because we hadn't had a losing season since he had come.

Even Dad had been caught up in the excitement with the thought that his boy would play for the man. It had been the only thing that seemed to make him happy, that and his drinking, which killed him.

Dad died in a car accident last year. He drove drunk without his lights in the dead of night and took a curve off into a ravine.

Next year, I would get my chance to play for Coach and see what all the fuss was about. I can't say I thought it was going to be fun. I had seen what Troy went through during the season.

I was in the eighth grade. The only time I had any direct dealings with Coach was when he came to pay respects at Dad's wake. Troy and I had escaped from the constant stream of visitors to play ball on our dirt court behind our small house.

We were playing horse when I shot from our make-shift free throw line and missed. It hit the rim and shot back over my head. I turned to retrieve it but stopped dead in my tracks.

Standing with the ball in his hands, Coach Carver smiled. He said, "Gotta get those free throws down, Dean. Can't win if you don't hit those."

This coming season was Troy's senior year. From listening to Troy and Freddie, I knew they had a strong team, but it would be a tough schedule with being in the center of basketball country.

"Gotta see this dog," Freddie said, patting the head of a young bluetick hound. "Buck here has a lot of promise."

"You said that about the last pup you were going to buy." Troy gave a laugh as he opened the passenger side door for me to scoot into the middle. "That dog took off, and it took us two days to run the darn thing down. Ran all the way across the bottom."

"I'll give ya I might have made a slight miscalculation on that one," Freddie pressed his lips together and shook his head. "I got him from Tucker. Should've known he don't know a thing about coon dogs. This one I got from Harris. I saw him up at the Hobo Station yesterday. He said if I like him, I can have him for fifty bucks."

"Fifty?" Troy lifted his eyebrow. "Buck here must be something special, but there's only one way to see. Let's try him out in the hollow past Pumpkin Hill."

On both sides of me, doors slammed. Freddie turned the ignition. For a brief moment, Freddie fell silent. I saw his mouth open, but no words came out. He had seen my shoes.

Freddie exchanged looks with Troy, who shrugged.

"What can I say? Dean hasn't taken them off since I gave them to him," Troy said, making light of my not wearing boots.

I just smiled wide.

The truth was that I had on Troy's old pair of Converses from playing ball when he had been a freshman. The shoes were still a little big for me and well-worn, but they were mine now.

Troy had told me I shouldn't wear them except on the court. I reckoned he was right, but there again, they were all I had.

My old shoes were too tight. Troy didn't have any other hand-me-downs that didn't have holes in the bottom of the sole.

Troy's boots came from his summer money made at Armstrong Feed Store. Our neighbor, Clyde Moore, worked there and helped Troy get the job. He would pick Troy up every morning. Otherwise, Troy wouldn't have had a way into Booneville, not with Momma needing our car to go to work at the factory.

Without another word, off we went on our adventure. At least, on *my* adventure. I had hunted with my brother too many times to count, but he had never let me go with his friends, and never, ever at midnight.

The woods in northeast Mississippi's foothills were flush with white-tail deer, raccoons, squirrels, and beaver. Labor Day brought dove season when the farmers seeded their fields to bring in their prey. With Thanksgiving came deer season when hunters braved early mornings and frigid temps to bag a buck.

Ponds had an abundance of catfish and spotted bass, which brought out turtles and snakes. Down at the pond behind our house, Troy had first taught me how to shoot. "Water moccasins slither on top of the water. Take into account they aren't moving straight and aim for the head."

Troy was the best shot I knew. I seldom saw him miss. He also was the one who taught me to treat a gun with respect.

"Assume it's loaded or don't pick it up," he told me.

Tonight, we weren't going out to shoot anything, though Freddie had his shotgun and rifle in his gun rack on his back window. From listening to the two talk, that's what had gone wrong last time.

As soon as Freddie fired the gun, the dog had taken off. This time, the plan was first to see if the dog could tree a coon before seeing if the dog was gun shy.

Troy thought he was some kind of expert with dogs because Coach Carver had told him a thing or two about training. Troy bragged that Coach could teach a dog to do most anything. I believed Troy.

Coach brought his German Shepherd, Skippy, with him most places except school. Many Saturday practices or during the summer, Skippy would come and stay out in the truck's bed. The dog would never move from his spot and waited patiently for Coach to return.

I don't know about anyone else, but that dog scared me. It was the way he looked at me like I was his next meal.

Freddie turned onto a side road and parked. Getting out of the truck, I was met with an eerie silence. Above us, the moon shone brightly while the tree branches swayed in the slight breeze.

Refusing to let them see my nervousness, I clicked on my flashlight as Troy had done. Freddie banged the side of the truck.

"Come on, Buck. Let's get going."

I jumped, and Troy laughed. At first, my pride was hurt, but not for long. With a quick look at Troy, I saw he wasn't laughing at me.

After hopping out of the truck, the dog sat there, wagging his tail as if waiting for a treat. Freddie motioned with his hand.

"Get on out there. Go get 'em," Freddie said, pointing to a trail opening into the woods. "Dagnabit!"

I had never gone coon hunting much but realized that the dog should have taken off. Instead of streaking into the woods, Buck walked around Freddie's legs, happy as you please.

Freddie wasn't pleased. He was mad.

Taking his hat off, he hit it against his leg. Freddie did everything he could think of to get that dog hunting. He even ran toward the woods hoping the dog would run into it. Buck ran happily alongside Freddie. When Freddie stopped, so did Buck. The poor dog seemed confused. The angrier Freddie got, the more Buck hopped around him.

"I'll tell you what, Freddie," Troy teased. "I'll betcha that if you showed him yourself how to catch a scent. If you get down…"

"Just shut up." Freddie threw his hands forward. "What do you want me to do?"

Troy exchanged looks with me, holding back laughter I saw in his eyes. He shrugged. "The good news is that old Buck there likes you…for sure." He drew in a chuckle. "Maybe he's been trained to tree people."

Freddie kicked the dirt. "He's young…and not used to me…"

"Maybe if we walk around for a while," I offered, afraid my night would end before it began. "Buck will pick up a scent."

I didn't wait for either of them to agree. I just started walking and ignored their squabbling.

There was something so peaceful and still walking through the woods at that time of night. All around me, the moonlight beams broke against the trees, giving off ominous shadows.

I confess that my bravery in the darkness was due to the knowledge that I wasn't alone. Otherwise, I wouldn't have been trekking around out there at midnight. In the distance, I heard an owl hoot. I also was aware of coyotes that roamed these woods.

Tonight, there wouldn't be much hunting. On the bright side, I wouldn't have to worry about predators attacking. We were making way too much noise. Freddie kept encouraging the dog to hunt while Troy ribbed Freddie.

Glancing over my shoulder, I saw Freddie shaking his head. Buck was going tree to tree, peeing on each. Abruptly, Freddie stopped dead in his tracks. Leaning over, he placed his hands on his knees and laughed.

Before long, all three of us were laughing so hard my side hurt.

"Looks like you will be saving yourself fifty bucks," Troy said. "That dog hasn't ever hunted."

"But he seems to love ya, Freddie. Might make ya a good dog to have around," I offered naively. "I mean, how often do ya go coon hunting?"

Rubbing his chin in thought, Freddie smiled. "What would I do with a bluetick hound that doesn't know how to track a scent?"

"The same as you would do now with basketball season on us."

Before Troy's voice died away, something caught my attention, flickering in the moonlight. I stared that way for a spell and then walked toward it.

At first, I thought it was an old can gleaming in a beam of light. I drew closer. In the middle of a small clearing, I saw some sort of silver container with coils hooked up to it. In the fire pit, there was only smoke billowing where once a fire burned.

Someone had put it out…a short time ago.

Immediately, I felt a hand grab my collar and almost lift me off my feet.

"Still," Troy whispered in my ear. "Run."

I didn't need to be told a second time. I took off. Tripping over a tree root, I scrambled back on my feet.

No one in their right mind would mess with a moonshine still. I thought any second, I would hear a gunshot.

In front of me, I saw Freddie's truck. No boy in the world could have been happier. Freddie was in front of me, sitting against his bumper to catch his breath.

Behind me, Troy said, "Get in."

I obeyed without a word. Taking a step into the truck, I had to laugh to myself. From the corner of my eye, I caught sight of Buck lying down in the truck's bed. The dog had beat us all back.

Relief flooded me as Freddie backed up and drove off in silence. It was only when he pulled up to let us out at our house that panic returned. I hadn't noticed in my hurry to get back to the truck, but I did now. I lost one of my shoes.

Chapter Two

The next morning, I watched Troy wake up from across the room. I was still in bed but hadn't slept much because I was worried about what to do about my shoes. He frowned. I knew he was irritated with me for going with him last night.

Our home was small and only had two bedrooms. We shared a room, which was tiny, but it could hold two twin beds.

We lived in Old Man Sanders' tenant house. He didn't use it anymore and rented it to Momma cheap. It was in desperate need of painting and repairs. Moreover, there wasn't any indoor plumbing. The outhouse was about a hundred yards from our back door. The screen door was torn, and the front steps had rotted.

In the winter, there was an awful draft. In the summer, it was like a furnace because we didn't have air conditioning.

"I thought about it all night." Troy sat up and hung his feet off the side of the bed. "You have two choices. You either wear your old shoes or mine with the holes in the soles. One thing we're not going to do is bother Momma with this. She has enough on her mind."

I nodded. I couldn't say I didn't know something was bothering Momma. When she wasn't working, she slept, and she never smiled anymore. I think it had something to do with the money Dad owed when he died.

Momma struggled to make ends meet for our family. She worked fifty hours a week at Brown Shoes, the local shoe factory in Booneville. It was the only money coming into our household even before Dad died.

Money had always been an issue as far back as I could remember. When Momma and Dad married, he had become a tenant farmer on Waylon Haney's farm, one of the county's largest cotton and soybean producers. Neither of them had graduated high school, but, according to Momma, they had done right well for a time.

When I was five, Vernon Barnes lost his right arm in a combine accident. Afterward, he never held a job. Dad spent most days drinking on the porch with his pack of hunting dogs, which amounted to no more than a bunch of mongrel hounds.

Momma said I would have liked the man he was before the accident. She would always talk about him like he had been. I can't say whether she spoke the truth or not. I didn't know that man. The man I knew had given me a black eye for not bringing him his beer quick enough.

"I reckon I'll wear my old ones," I said finally. "Momma will think they still fit."

"It'll work for now," Troy agreed. "I'll figure something out. Know though, you're going to have to wear them all day. We're going over to Grandpa Barnes after church."

Most Sundays, we went over to Grandma Taylor's. Grandma had lived with us after Grandpa Taylor passed away from a heart attack. The house had been crowded, and Troy slept on the couch, but then Grandma developed diabetes and lost her leg. At that point, Grandma went to live with her sister, my Great-Aunt Ruth, no more than a mile down the road.

Until Troy mentioned it, I had forgotten we were going over to visit Dad's family. Grandpa and Grandmother

Barnes invited us over to celebrate Troy's birthday. We were going to have fried chicken and cake.

I thought it was a little strange. Troy's birthday was a month ago. I mean, my birthday was in a couple of weeks. Troy told me not to say a word about it because it would be rude.

If I was honest with myself, I reckoned I was a little jealous of my brother. I felt the Barnes side favored Troy more than me. Troy looked more like a Barnes with his thick dark hair and dark eyes, and he wasn't that tall. None of the Barnes ever got over six feet, but Momma expected I would be taller than Troy. I was at his same height now despite him being four years older.

I looked more like Momma's side. I had mousy brown hair with the most annoying cowlick. My eyes weren't nearly as dark as Troy's. They were more of a hazel that lightened and darkened depending on what I wore.

We hadn't seen much of that side of the family since Dad died. Grandpa had a small farm over in Thrasher. Most times, though, I enjoyed going. Uncle Orson and Aunt Maude had built their house on the other side of Grandpa's driveway. I enjoyed playing with our cousins, Rachel and Ernie.

Rachel was a year older than me; Ernie, two years younger. Most of the time, we would play basketball. They had a nice dirt court behind their house. I imagined that was what we would do today. From what I had heard, Rachel was on varsity at Thrasher and was pretty good.

Like I predicted, Momma didn't give my shoes a second look. Matter of fact, she didn't say much about anything either going to church or afterward at my grandparents.

Thrasher wasn't a long ride from New Site, no more than twenty minutes. My grandparents had a simple whitewashed house with a long porch out front. I liked to swing on the porch swing when I had been younger.

Grandmother Barnes had gone all out for the meal. The chicken tasted mighty good along with the mashed potatoes and gravy.

I hadn't even taken my second bite when the conversation turned to basketball. I kept eating.

Grandpa Barnes was a short man who walked with a limp due to the fact one leg was an inch shorter than the other. He had boots to correct the birth defect, but he never wore them.

His thinning hair was slicked back. He sat at the head of the table and gestured for Troy to sit on his left; Uncle Orson was on his right. I was seated at the end beside Momma.

"Eager for a new season?" Grandpa Barnes asked.

Troy put his fork down. Evidently, he was preparing for a long talk.

New Site and Thrasher were county rivals. Moreover, Prentiss County was renown as basketball country.

"Coach Carver is excited for the season to begin. Everyone is anticipating a great year for us." Troy smiled. "This being the first year that they have classified four divisions for the state tournament."

"Going for the first B title, are you?" Uncle Orson asked, taking a sip of his iced tea. "Guess I wouldn't expect more from that cocky son-of-a-gun coach of yours."

"Orson!" Grandpa Barnes reprimanded him. "It's no different than Thrasher going for the BB title."

Uncle Orson grinned broadly. He was a younger version of Grandpa Barnes; except he had no limp. He had one of those personalities that made you want to be his friend. Momma said Uncle Orson could charm you, but you couldn't trust him. I supposed then he was in the right profession. He was a used-car salesman.

"Just saying that Carver always has something up his sleeves."

"Coach Carver is the smartest coach around," Troy said defensively. He had lost his smile. Someone had questioned the almighty Coach Joe Carver.

"You might think that," Uncle Orson kept the argument going. "but what coach takes his team off the court of a tie game and won't play overtime? Scared to lose if you ask me."

I knew immediately Uncle Orson was talking about playing Booneville last year.

When Troy had been a sophomore, Booneville Blue Devils had been the powerhouse of the state with a player that was a quarter inch shy of seven feet. Before New Site played them, Booneville had won all their games by at least thirty points.

I had been there when the Royals had played the Blue Devils that year. Our team looked like dwarfs compared to Booneville. On our first possession, Troy dribbled into one of the corners of the court and slowed down the game. It had given us a chance to win, but we had fallen short. We lost by a point, 17-16.

It was the closest anyone came to Booneville that year. The Blue Devils went undefeated and won the A-AA crown.

They were still undefeated when the Royals met up with them last year. Matter of fact, Booneville had been going for a record-breaking consecutive streak that night. Troy said that there wasn't even standing room in the gym it was so packed. Everyone had come to see Booneville break the winning streak.

I hadn't gotten to go to the game. Troy had told me how the Royals were losing but staged a dramatic comeback to tie the game at the final buzzer. Afterward, Troy ran back to the bench, thinking Coach Carver would tell them how to win the game. Instead, Coach told the boys to get dressed. At first, Troy thought Coach was kidding. He wasn't.

With the stands still packed, the Royals dressed, walked out of the packed gym, and went to eat at Jack Sprat. I reckoned Booneville was still mad about that one.

"No, sir," Troy replied. "The rule stated that a team doesn't have to play overtime. Coach said that he wasn't going to let Booneville set the record against us."

"Wasn't right," Uncle Orson countered. "Ended their streak."

"We went by the rules."

"The rule was changed this year, wasn't it?"

"It's what I hear," Troy said. "Doesn't change the fact that we didn't do anything wrong. Coach knows the rules better than the refs."

Uncle Orson chuckled. "I've seen him with that worn-out rulebook in his back pocket."

"Coach Carver has never been wrong about anything he questions."

Our uncle didn't have a response. Mainly because Troy was right.

Looking up from my meal, I studied Troy's face. To him, Coach Carver was the best coach around. I'd give him the fact that Coach Carver had turned the Royals basketball program around.

The Royals had only won three games combined over the last two years prior to Coach Carver appearance. Since that time, the Royals hadn't had a losing season and wasn't the laughingstock of the county anymore. Each year, their record got better.

Coach Carver put a team on the court that was well-disciplined and prepared. He expected everyone to do their part. He would do his. Troy said that Coach always told them, "You don't get on the court except to win."

This year at school, there was growing anticipation. Big changes had occurred in the high school basketball playoffs. A new format had been established. Each division got its own title: B, BB, A, and AA. The week after the

State titles were won, a tournament would commence for the overall crown for the state called the Grand Slam.

My opinion was guarded about the changes. Granted, the State B title would seem to be attainable, but I didn't know how a small school was supposed to be able to compete with schools so much larger in the Grand Slam. It seemed an impossible task for a school our size or any B school for that matter.

New Site was a small rural community made up mostly of farmers. Our school had just over a hundred students total in the high school. We didn't have a football or baseball team. Yet, the Royals lived for basketball.

"Give Coach Carver his due, Orson," Grandpa Barnes chuckled. "You're still upset when he beat ya in high school."

Uncle Orson grimaced as well as I expected he might. It was common knowledge how good Coach Joe Carver had been as a basketball player himself. He had been an All-State guard at Marietta when they had won State. He continued playing ball at Northeast Junior College and then at Mississippi State, where he had been SEC All-Conference. Afterward, he had joined the Marines.

Rachel picked up her plate. "I'm done. Wanna go play some ball instead of talking about it?"

I was more than ready. I helped Ernie and her clean the table. Then, we headed out back to play ball.

Chapter Three

I regretted playing ball with my cousins the next morning. My heels had blistered and bled.

My chores still had to be done before school which wouldn't have been a big deal if it had been only mine. I was supposed to clean the kitchen, cook if need be, and wash the clothes. Most could easily be done after school. Most mornings, we ate a bowl of cereal. So, cleaning up the bowls wasn't a big deal.

Troy's chores were a different matter. Last year, Troy had started paying me twenty-five cents a week from his summer money to do his when the team started practicing for the season. I didn't mind feeding the animals and collecting the eggs from the chickens. It was how I got money to go to the games. This morning, though, my feet hurt so bad I did them barefooted.

Coming back in from the barn, I saw Troy racing out the front door to catch his ride with Freddie. I called out, "Troy, wait. What am I supposed to do?"

Looking back at me, my brother stopped in his tracks. He sighed and rubbed his forehead. "I don't think you have a choice. You're going to hafta wear your old shoes. Get through the day and…"

"And we'll go to Booneville this afternoon to buy some new sneakers? I saw Grandmother Barnes slip you a five-dollar bill…that was besides the ten in your birthday card. I'll figure out a way to pay you back."

A pained look crossed his face. Then, he nodded. "Yeah, we'll do that. I'll call Grandma Taylor to see if we can get her car."

"What's the matter?"

He shook his head. "Nothing…it's fine."

But it wasn't. I could tell. "Did you have plans for that money?"

"It's nothing," he said. "I'll call Missy and cancel."

"Missy? Who's Missy?" I had never heard the name and hadn't a clue who it was. "A date…you have a date?"

"Yeah… maybe. It's no big deal."

I had known Troy dated, but he usually didn't during the season. Coach Carver called girlfriends a distraction.

Freddie beeped his horn. Troy gestured he was coming.

I felt bad. It was my fault, not Troy's, I lost my shoe.

"Go ahead," I said. "I'll call Grandma when I get home. She might have an old pair of Grandpa's or something."

Troy nodded and gave me a small smile. "Don't say anything at school. We don't want nobody's pity."

"I won't," I promised, but I knew it would be hard.

Cramming my foot into my old shoes, they hurt so bad, but I did it determined to make it through the day. Troy always looked after me. I didn't want to embarrass him.

I limped onto the bus and sat beside Larry. I reckoned he was my best friend. We had gone to school together since the first grade and played basketball together.

"What happened to you? Did ya hurt your foot?"

"Just a blister." I shrugged him off and changed the subject to basketball.

Getting to school, I let Larry go in front of me and took the steps down with care. Gritting my teeth, I hurried to catch up with him under the breezeway.

Outside the doors, I caught sight of Coach Carver talking with the high school principal. Tall and lanky, Mr.

Jones wore his usual dark suit and tie. An older man, he had combed his hair to the side in an effort to hide his thinning hair. Pushing his wire-rimmed glasses back up his nose, he nodded toward us.

Mr. Jones was a kind man, but I had no desire to call his attention to me. Nobody wanted to get called to the principal's office, not even his. It was rumored that Mr. Jones had been influential in getting Coach Carver to coach here. He was his uncle.

Coach Carver had been coaching in Laurel before he had returned to Prentiss County. I had heard that Coach came home to be close to family and help on his dad's farm. He had given up a job at an AA school to coach here. Seems family was important to him. I had seen his wife and children at every game I had attended.

Not wanting to interrupt their conversation, I lowered my gaze, but Coach Carver wouldn't let us walk by without a greeting.

"Good morning, Dean. Larry."

"Morning, Coach," we said in unison.

Coach Carver smiled, one of those knowing smiles. The kind that made you feel that he could look deep in your soul and know everything you had done or thought. Athletically built, Coach stood at six feet. His dark hark was cut in a marine-style crew-cut, and he had piercing blue eyes.

When he spoke, his voice carried the confidence and authority of a marine. He had earned it. He had served in the marine corps after college.

"Ready for the season to begin?"

Nodding repeatedly, I managed to find my voice, "Yes, sir."

Larry and I continued to homeroom. I'll admit I had a spring in my step after Coach acknowledged us. There was something about feeling like you belong.

Troy felt it and took pride in being a Royal. My brother wore his red and white letter jacket with NS on the left side alongside his teammates.

It was widely known Coach never cut a player as long as you were willing to work hard but playing for Coach wasn't easy. Any of his players could attest to the grinding drills and the demanded commitment.

Troy had learned the hard way about how hard it was to play for Coach Carver. He had been so excited to finally play for Coach, but it had only taken one practice for Troy to doubt whether he could become a Royal.

Coach ran his practice like boot camp. He was on you from the time you stepped on the court until you ran the last suicide. Coach wanted your best at all times.

I remembered Troy sneaking into the house after his first practice so Dad wouldn't see him. My brother didn't want to tell Dad he just couldn't do it.

He threw his practice bag on the floor. His face still reddened; his clothes drenched in sweat.

"I'm done," he declared. "I can't do this. Coach didn't let up…he ran us into the ground. I'm handing back my stuff in the morning."

"What about Dad?" I asked because I would have been more afraid of Dad than a basketball practice. Dad had talked of nothing else except Troy playing for Coach Carver.

"I just can't do it."

I had never seen Troy so disheartened when he left the next morning for school. With his hopes to play basketball dashed, he planned on quitting. I begged him not to give it up. Honestly, it wasn't him playing ball that worried me. I was frightened for him when Dad found out.

Turned out, Troy had another obstacle to overcome. He had to hand in his bag to Coach.

The story of Troy going to Coach's class went around the school. It's probably still told. Troy knocked on

Coach's door while Coach was teaching his history class. When Coach came to the door, Troy extended his hand with his bag.

With his eyes lowered, Troy said, "I'm sorry, Coach. I just can't…"

Coach shut the door, leaving Troy standing in the hall with the bag in his hand. Troy knocked again.

This time, Troy looked Coach in the eyes. "I'm sorry…"

Giving Troy one of his looks, Coach interrupted my brother, "Practice is at 3:00."

Once more, Coach closed the door.

Troy was at practice at 3:00.

Practices didn't change. From what I saw, they were still as brutal, but the funny thing was, over time, Troy didn't complain. What once was unthinkable had become second nature.

I heard that was the way it was playing for Coach. I wanted to play basketball, but I questioned my own ability to play for the man. I told myself I didn't have to worry about it until next year.

Like my brother, I believed we were going to have a great year. The junior high team consisted of both seventh- and eighth-graders. Thirteen out of the twenty boys in the lower grades played on the team. Besides Larry Ross, I played with J.C. Ward and Vergil Davis for as long as I could remember.

There may not have been many of us, but we all had one desire: to play for New Site.

Practice was during second period. One thing about playing at a small school was that I knew everyone well. We had played together since we started school.

Coach Douglas was the middle school coach. This was his first year teaching fresh out of college. He tried to imitate Coach Carver, but we all knew it wasn't the same.

Coach Douglas didn't push us as Coach Carver would have.

After changing into my gym clothes, I was the first one in line to do lay-ups. Dribbling down to the basket, I lifted my right foot and laid the ball into the basket. I came down in pain.

My foot throbbed. It hurt so bad. Practice didn't go well. I was slow on defense. It wasn't only J. C. moving around me with ease; it was everybody. I took pride in my defense. I may not have been the biggest man on the court or best shooter, but nobody got around me, until today.

Troy had taught me not to look at the ball, but the belly of my opponent. *The belly never moves,* and *always be on your toes. If you're flatfooted, they will go around you every time.*

"Dean," Coach Douglas called me out. "Go sit down. When you decide to play, let me know."

Deflated and embarrassed, I walked over to the bench. I wanted to play, but my feet wouldn't cooperate. They ached so bad. Fighting back the tears I swore no one would see me cry, I took off my right sneaker. My foot had bled through the sock on the heel and ball of my foot.

"Dean, come with me."

I looked up to see Coach Carver in front of me.

"Don't bother putting back on your shoe."

A tear escaped down my cheek. Quickly, I wiped it back in hopes that he didn't see my weakness as I hobbled behind him.

He brought me into the high school's team locker room. "Sit down. Pull off your other shoe and let me see your feet."

I obeyed and lifted them up on the bench. In silence, Coach took out a first-aid kit and applied a salve and Band-Aids on my blisters.

Afterward, he got up and went into the equipment room. He came back with a box.

"See if these fit."

I swallowed hard, opening the box. They were brand new Converse high tops. They were mine.

Chapter Four

The New Site Royals basketball season was about to begin. I had been ready for an hour to leave, but I had to wait for Momma. We were going to the game.

Away games were challenging for me to go to, especially on a school night. Momma worked at least five days a week, and also usually Saturday mornings. With Momma working like she did, I wouldn't have a ride, but tonight, even though it was a Tuesday, Momma was going to Burnsville.

She had come home from work, intent on going to see her eldest play ball. For supper, Troy and I had a glass of cornbread and milk. Troy didn't want anything too heavy. I was just so excited. Besides, I planned on grabbing a bag of popcorn at the concession stand.

Momma had skipped supper and taken a bath. She didn't have to worry about Troy. He caught a ride with Freddie to the team bus.

Realizing how crowded the gym was going to be, I wanted to leave before Troy. We were still there after Freddie and Troy drove off. I pressed Momma.

"We need to hurry. We won't get a seat."

"Calm down," Momma said as she walked out into the living room.

She looked pretty dressed in an old plaid jumper, white shirt, and a cardigan sweater. Her hair was teased and curled and red lipstick on her lips. She was done up real nice with a big smile on her face.

I hadn't seen Momma smile in ever so long.

Driving over to the game, I forgot all about how my Momma looked. I grew anxious we wouldn't get in to see the game. My anxiety only grew worse when we turned into the parking lot. It was packed.

Thankfully, Momma finally found a parking space. Pulling back on the street, we parked on the side of a ditch. Getting out of the car, I ran ahead of Momma.

"Slow down," she called.

I didn't. Instead, I rushed to get in line. Momma caught up with me before I was asked to pay, which was a good thing. I only had a quarter in my pocket for popcorn.

Glancing over my shoulder, I was pleased that we had made it inside. There was a long line behind us. I felt Momma's hand on my shoulder as we walked through the lobby into the smoke-filled gym.

The girls were just warming up. Sitting on the bleachers behind the girls' bench was our boys' team, including Troy. They sat together, not with friends and especially not with any of their girlfriends.

Troy sat in-between Freddie and Donnie Morris, the seniors on the team. Donnie played center. He was tall, standing six-four, and had a devil of a shot. Troy was a guard and brought up the ball. Behind them, Jimmy Massey and Earl Bailey, both forwards, sat with Barry Perkins, the other guard.

Coach Carver didn't label his players, but, I reckoned, Donnie was our best player. He had wavy light brown hair and blue eyes, which seemed to attract girls.

Donnie always had some pretty girl by his side. It had gotten him in trouble last year with Coach Carver's rules.

At the Turkey Tournament over at Wheeler, Donnie hadn't ridden the bus to the game. Instead, he had his girlfriend drive him over. Coach didn't play him. Coach didn't even let him dress. Donnie got mad and quit.

The move stunned me. I couldn't believe that Coach let his best player just go. I realized that Coach Carver was adamant about his rules, but, I mean, how did Coach think we were going to win without Donnie.

When I had told Troy Coach should let Donnie come back, Troy told me what, I was certain, Coach had told him. "It wouldn't be fair for everyone else to work hard and follow training and not Donnie."

Troy said that Coach's rules were for everyone. It didn't matter who it was.

Donnie quitting caused quite a stir at school. For me, I didn't see the harm if Coach made an exception, just once. We needed Donnie to win.

Yet, it was Donnie who wanted to come back. He had even come over to the house to talk with Troy about the situation.

The two sat on the front porch and held a deep discussion. Sitting in the living room, I heard every word. The window didn't close shut and the walls weren't insulated.

"Coach has all these stupid rules," Donnie fumed. "Can't drink soda! Can't eat candy! Cut your hair. Runs us in the ground. What about the curfew? He even comes by our houses to check on us. He doesn't trust us. What kind of coach does that?"

"A coach that wins, Donnie. He does the same thing for all of us. This isn't on Coach, but you."

"I think I've done something dumb," Donnie said.

"Then go to Coach," Troy urged.

Donnie had. No one knew what was said at the meeting between Coach Carver and Donnie, but after running an extra fifty laps, Donnie was back on the team. He had taken his punishment, which I admired.

It must have taken a lot of courage to face Coach and admit you were wrong. Troy said that he didn't see anyone work harder than Donnie after he came back.

At the moment, Donnie was leaning over and talking to Troy. Troy laughed.

From the corner of my eye, I saw Larry and J.C., waving at me to join them. Not wanting to leave Momma alone, I hesitated.

She gestured for me to go ahead. "I see Mrs. Morton. I'll sit by her."

I didn't need anything else. I bolted toward Larry and plopped down beside him. Then, we waited while the girls played. I tried to watch, but their different rules drove me crazy. I watched as one of our girls pulled down a rebound, dribbled up to the center court line, stopped, and threw it to one of our other players on the other side of the line.

The rover was the only one who could go both ways. Honestly, the girls' rules confused and frustrated me to watch a player gain momentum and stop at the line and pass the ball to someone on the other side.

My cousin Rachel felt the same way. She said it was stupid to treat girls differently. I couldn't argue with her on that one. Watching the game was like watching a pot boil though I would get kicked in the shin if I admitted that to Rachel.

At half-time, the whole boys' team rose and went into the *Away* locker room in unison—a signal for me to answer my belly. Popcorn called.

Larry and I went to the concession stand along with half the gym. It seemed like everyone else had the same idea. Didn't bother me. We mingled with other kids from school who came to support the team while we waited.

By the time we got back to our seats, there wasn't much left of the game or my popcorn. I counted down in my head until the buzzer rang. The girls dispersed. I couldn't even tell you who won the game.

My eyes were on Troy. He had the ball under his arms readied to come out on the floor with the team behind him.

There was something magical about the start of a season—the anticipation of possibilities filled the air. Nothing was out of our reach. Watching the red and white charge onto the court, I felt goosebumps emerge on my arms.

The gym exploded. Cheers went up on both sides. As much as we expected a win tonight, Burnsville wanted nothing more than to spoil our dreams.

Class B, Burnsville was a small school itself but was larger than we were. They were situated north of us in Tishomingo County.

Coach Carver walked the sideline during warm-ups with his red towel in hand. He constantly talked to the players until the game started. Only then did he take a seat. Clean cut and disciplined, the starting five lined up for the tip-off.

Donnie jumped off against his opponent and knocked the ball back to Troy. Setting up in a three-man rotation, Troy threw it over to Barry on the left side. Donnie cut through the middle where Barry hit him, and then Donnie laid it up and through the net.

The game had begun; the season had begun.

My hope had been that the team would pick up where they left off last year. It didn't happen. The rust of their summer break showed. Troy's pass was a second late; Barry seemed a step off with his defense. Donnie wasn't getting his shot off quick enough.

The clock wound down. To my surprise, the game was closer than I had expected. With time for only one more shot, the game was tied. Troy dribbled up over mid-court and threw it over to Donnie. Donnie faked to the left and went right. He hit a jump shot to win the game.

Relief flooded me, and I could breathe again. Not pretty, but it was a win.

Besides, Troy played a solid game. He was a guard. As a senior, Troy seemed to be the leader on the team. He didn't score big numbers but brought the ball down and called the plays Coach wanted.

Afterward, I stood for a moment and watched the bleachers clear. The court filled quickly with fans talking about the game and players slowly making their way to their locker room. Larry and J.C. had already taken off when I caught sight of Momma.

Stepping off the bleachers, two young boys came by, almost knocking me on the ground. I turned backward for a second, wondering whether to shout at them or not. I decided not to yell. Momma was too close.

I took a step back and ran into someone myself. Turning, I gasped, seeing it was the Burnsville basketball coach talking to one of the officials. I said, "Sorry."

The man waved me off politely, paying me no mind. He was engrossed in his conversation. "Almost had them tonight, but we'll get them next week for sure at New Site. Gonna take the paint off the building."

Not thinking much of it, I moved around the Burnsville coach to see Coach Carver standing next to Mr. Jones, who was talking to him. Coach Carver didn't seem to be listening. His eyes were on the Burnsville coach.

Giving Coach a smile, I walked toward Momma. Coach stepped in my path.

Tilting his head toward the Burnsville coach, Coach asked, "Dean, did you hear Coach White say that they were coming to our gym next week to take the paint off the building?"

"Yes, sir," I replied.

There was a subtle change in his expression. If I wasn't mistaken, I believed that Coach Carver took that as a challenge.

I wasn't wrong.

The next Tuesday came, and Burnsville came calling. After a Friday night win against East Union, Troy said their practices had been centered on whether they would let anyone come into their gym and take the paint off the building.

From the way Troy looked, walked, and talked, I was glad I wasn't from Burnsville. Troy was angry. More importantly, he was focused.

From the first jump ball, New Site began its attack, fierce and unmerciful. This was a battle that the Royals had no intention of losing. After Donnie made his first shot, Burnsville went to throw the ball back in but was hit hard with an intense one-two-two press.

Burnsville didn't have an answer to the defense. Confused and dazed, the Burnsville boys limped back into their locker room, losing 50 to 12.

It was half-time.

Chapter Five

The gray days of December were upon us. Yet it might as well have been the hot sunshine of late August, the way people were acting.

The gloom and misery of the rains and fog hadn't dampened people's spirits in New Site. I had never seen everyone being so friendly to each other. Smiles seemed to be plastered on their faces. Momma was even happy.

Momma and I hadn't missed a game. Despite the hours she was putting in at the factory, she hadn't made an excuse about not going, whether home or away. Her boy and his team were the talk of the county.

As of late, her pride in Troy was evident in most all she said and did. The thought that my older brother was her favorite had occurred to me, and I'll admit I might have been a tad jealous over that fact.

My team had done well itself. With having grown a few inches over the summer, Coach Douglas had moved me over to the wing. The move took me out of my game a little. I was used to playing guard like Troy. I felt like I didn't have the control I had before. Now I had to get used to focusing on shooting, but I couldn't complain. We hadn't lost.

Momma hadn't been able to come to any of my games. I reckoned it bothered me. Then I reasoned that Troy was a senior, and my team was only a junior high team. I couldn't go wallowing in self-pity; anything that brought the smile back to her face was a good thing.

The Royals had won eight straight games. I'd hafta say that school was going well for me. Coach Carver had begun to let us eighth graders sit in on practice if we had our homework done.

Mine was always complete before the last bell rang. Larry and the other guys made fun of me for being a teacher's pet, but I didn't mind. Momma said she never had to worry about me and grades. I always got straight A's.

When Troy had been younger, Momma had struggled with him to get his schoolwork done. That ended when he got to high school; Troy had to make passing grades, or he wouldn't get to play ball.

Sitting in the gym, my buddies and I watched the high schoolers practice in silence. No one dared cut up while Coach ran the guys through the drills.

The first thing that had struck me was how hard they played at a practice. No one just ran through a drill. Everyone played like they were in a game. Finally, Coach blew his whistle, signaling the end. It was time to run.

Coach took a seat in the bleachers with a whistle in his mouth as the team lined up on the line to run. Blowing sporadically, Coach had the guys run, starting and stopping on each tweet. On the sidelines, the manager, Stuart sat with a stopwatch in hand.

I sat behind Stuart and watched as he picked up a pencil to make a mark by anyone's name that was late crossing the line. They would have to run an extra lap.

After the last whistle, Coach stood with the whistle hanging from his hand. Some of the boys collapsed to the floor, others walked around, and a few bent over, catching their breath. Coach had run them hard, but we all knew that no team was in better shape.

In the stands, a few of the fathers, along with some of the loyal fans, had watched practice, too. It seemed the activity was almost like a game for people around here. Coach allowed visitors inside as long as he wasn't preparing for a particular team. Besides, this was a Friday night without a game.

There had been a small break without a game since Thanksgiving. The next one scheduled wasn't until Monday night against Kossuth.

"Good run today, boys." Coach Carver moved beneath the basket and looked at his watch. "We don't have long. Drink down your water and get changed. We need to leave if we want to get there before the game starts."

The team was going to watch Kossuth play Biggersville. For me, I wasn't that interested in the game, but Troy said I could go with him. I couldn't pass that up.

"Think of it like payback. You've covered for me with my chores since season started. I'm going with Freddie and his dad. He said you could come with us."

I didn't hesitate to agree. Troy gave me a whole list of rules to follow, mainly not to bother him; that, I could do.

Coach wanted his boys to see what they were up against come Monday. From my point of view, I didn't know if that was such a good idea, not from what I heard about the team.

Kossuth was an AA school. Not that Kossuth was much bigger than our community, but they drew from the surrounding area, which added to their attendance. This year, they had an overpowering team. Their shortest starter was six-three, their tallest, six-eight.

Driving over to the game, I hadn't the foggiest idea where we were going. Kossuth wasn't far off of the main highway. There again, the rain made the night darker. It was downpouring.

By the time we got to the gym, the parking lot was packed. We had to park across the road from the high school. Having only worn a flannel over my clothes, I was drenched by the time I got into the gym.

I stepped inside, shook off the rain the best I could, and followed my brother as the guys made their way up a side aisle of the *Visitors* side. Coach Carver sat in front of us with a friend of his.

Troy knew him. I think Troy called him Coach Tilman, but I don't know what team he coached because he seemed to be around our team a lot.

True to my word, I tried not to bother Troy and just observe, but it was near impossible to ignore the guys. Troy didn't seem to mind. He sat on my left side with Freddie beside him. Freddie goodheartedly teased me until Kossuth took the floor.

Then, the boys quieted. In silence, they watched a dominating Kossuth team play. From the beginning, Kossuth ate up the other team with their zone defense. The intimidating big men stole any pass inside and blocked most of the shots that Biggersville got off. On offense, they made it look easy. With repetitive precision, their players launched one easy lay-up after another.

Freddie eased over beside me. "Man, this team is tough. Don't you think? This will be one game I won't mind staying on the bench."

After another blocked shot, Freddie went on, "Did you see that? Out of nowhere! How ya gonna get a shot off? Even if you get round one of 'em, here comes another."

"For God's sake, Freddie! Shut up!" Donnie snapped.

Freddie was as funny as all get out, but I reckoned right now the team wanted to concentrate on the team they were going to play Monday night. Freddie scooted back and gave me a shrug. A moment later, he dug in his pocket.

"Why don't you run down and get me some gum and popcorn?"

After that, I spent the second quarter running up and down with concessions for the boys. Getting up for the third time, I noticed a couple of boys about my age across the way, pointing at me and laughing.

I didn't think much about it until I got in line again. At the concession stand, the woman must have thought I had a hole in my stomach as much popcorn as I was getting. Seeing me again, she gave me a small smile.

"Back for more, I see," she said, reaching for the popcorn before I asked.

"Yes, ma'am," I replied. "Two please and an orange soda."

Laying the money down, I took my order and turned into a gang of boys. The leader of the group looked to be about my age, but stouter and a tad taller. He grinned at me like a possum in a chicken coop with a missing front tooth.

"Where ya think yer going?"

"Back to my seat." I felt their eyes on me, but I didn't want no trouble. "Now, if you could get out of my way."

No one moved for me. Instead, the boys stepped closer.

"Ya from New Site?"

"Of course, he is. Look at him," another said. Standing by the first one, he was about the same height with the exact same look in his eyes. He was looking for trouble. "He's no bigger than a minnow in a pond and too big for his britches."

"Nothing more than a country hick."

I said nothing but tried to move around them. Someone shoved me. I tripped over a foot that extended in my path and fell flat on the floor.

Popcorn was scattered all over the place, and the soda splattered over me. I had worn my best blue buttoned-down. My shirt was now doused in orange.

Crawling back on my knees, I heard the horn blow signaling half-time. All around me, I heard people snicker. From behind the counter, the nice lady rushed to me with a wet cloth.

"Don't worry," she said, wiping my shirt. "It should come right out in a wash."

From the corner of my eye, I saw the boys laughing. My blood boiled. Anger rose inside of me like a raging bull ready to charge. All I could see was red.

Unconsciously, I rose back on my feet, ready to lunge toward the source of my humiliation. Suddenly, I felt a hand swat the back of my head.

"Don't do it, boy."

I looked back over my shoulder. Coach Carver.

He stood there just staring at me…like I had done something wrong. To my horror, I fought back tears. I was so mad.

"Here, son." The lady had already replaced my order. "No charge."

"Thank you, ma'am," I replied, glaring over at the boys. They had taken off, probably left the gym. Only that thought gave me pleasure.

Coach Carver stood behind me. I'm sure he was intimidating to them with his marine style crew cut and eyes that seemed to burn into you.

But it wasn't enough. I wanted them to pay.

When I returned to my seat, no one said a word. I did catch Troy exchanging a look with Donnie, but otherwise, nothing. The thrill of coming with the team vanished. I just wanted it to be over.

The rain had lightened, but my spirits hadn't. When we got home, Troy told me not to worry about it. He had my back. "Let it go. They're not worth it."

Easy for him to say. Star point guard on an undefeated team, good-looking, and popular at school. The girls loved him. Momma said Troy had charisma.

I hadn't been born so lucky. My eyes were so small that when I smiled, it looked like I had closed them. Troy had large brown eyes with long eyelashes. He would get so mad at me when I told him they looked like a girl's.

Troy had always had girls calling him. That was until he started dating this Missy, who I had yet to meet. I just had to endure the two of them talking on the phone late into the night.

I couldn't even find the courage to talk to one in class. I swore they didn't know I was alive. Sometimes I heard *nerd* behind my back, which I didn't understand.

I got good grades, sure, and mostly I didn't have to study for them. But I didn't wear glasses, nor did I carry around my books under my arms. Not to mention, I lived for basketball. Nerds didn't play ball.

Sleep didn't come easy. In the morning, I woke to the smell of bacon. Troy had cooked me breakfast: eggs, bacon, and biscuits. Troy didn't cook often, and when he did…well, usually it wasn't that good. Once, I bounced his biscuits off the floor.

This morning, it was like heaven.

Momma had already gone to work. The fact that Troy had gotten up early and cooked, meant something: *He feels sorry for me*. But I didn't care how bad he was in the kitchen. I was hungry.

"Like it, huh?" Troy said. "Told you I was a good cook."

Laughing, I almost choked on my first bite of eggs. "The question is, who are you? Because you aren't my brother."

Troy smiled real big and sat down with his plate. "Funny boy. We have a busy day today. You're coming to practice with me, so eat up. We have to feed the chickens."

My dark mood lifted by the time Freddie picked us up for practice. I couldn't help but laugh at Freddie's jokes, no matter how lame.

I shot around on the opposite end of the court while the guys warmed up. I refused to look at Coach when he came into the gym. I was still mad. *He should have stood up for me.*

When Coach whistled, I noticed that the boys took to the bleachers instead of continuing practice. I did the same so as not to make any noise to distract from Coach's speech.

"Well, boys, you got to see Kossuth. What did you think?"

A few fidgeted around, but no one answered. Coach didn't look like he expected any. He went on, walking back and forth in front of the boys, swinging his whistle around in one hand. In his other, he held coffee in a Styrofoam cup.

"We will have our hands full. They are tall and drive hard to the basket, but this is what we are going to do. We are going to play our game. We get one point ahead of this team, and we will beat them, and this is how we're going to do it."

Coach walked over to his blackboard and started drawing out his four-corner offense.

"They play a two-three zone. They're big." He pointed to the far-right corner, then the left. "We are going to spread them out. They will have to go man-to-man. When they do, we will beat them. This should give you an opportunity, Donnie. You will have Landry on you."

Everyone knew Coach was talking about Ray Landry, the six-eight star center. All eyes fell on Donnie.

"Yes, sir, Coach," Donnie answered assuredly.

At the moment, I noticed a definite difference in the guys' demeanor. It was as if all their worries and fears about not being able to beat Kossuth vanished.

The thought hit me. The team held this complete belief in their Coach. His word was gospel as was their belief in him. Coach had deemed Kossuth beatable. So, in turn, did they.

The team hit the practice court with a bounce in their step.

I had intended to continue to shoot around during their practice. Instead, I watched differently than I had before. I saw each player intent on what Coach told them. The second string acted as Kossuth on offense and defense.

"Barry," Coach directed. "Turn to your left. Landry always turns left to shoot."

The practice was long and hard, but not one of the guys seemed to mind. Whistle in hand, Coach took to the stands to run the team. I scooted down to Stuart to wait until it was over, intent on leaving with Troy.

Stuart stood to step down. I followed, but over my shoulder, I saw Coach Carver gesturing to me. I didn't want to go over but didn't have much of a choice.

Sighing, I stepped up a row and slid down beside Coach. He gave me a small smile.

"So, Dean, do you think we have a shot against Kossuth?"

I'm sure I looked confused. Despite the fact that I wanted us to beat Kossuth in the worst way, the odds were against us. They were so big.

Shrugging, I answered with a question. "Do you think we can win?"

His left eyebrow rose slightly like he was letting me in on a secret. "It doesn't matter what I believe. It's important what the boys believe."

The reply made me think for a moment. Biting my bottom lip, I said, "I suppose so."

"Belief is a powerful force," Coach stated, clapping his hands together. "The boys need to believe in themselves like I believe in them. If they do, we will win."

"I guess."

"You're mad at me. Aren't you, Dean?"

Stunned that he had noticed, I could only stare. *The man could read my mind.*

"You know that those Kossuth boys might have been laughing, but we weren't."

I nodded my head. "Yeah, I know. I saw." My voice must have conveyed my anger. I wasn't very good at disguising it.

"You think that I should have called those boys out or let you go at them," Coach said. "But ask yourself what good it would have done. Stupid follows stupid."

"Don't know what that means, Coach."

"It means that just because somebody does something stupid, you don't have to go down to their level. Sometimes it's better to let stupid be." He tilted his head and looked straight in my eyes. "Look, son, it takes a bigger man to walk away. They were trying to bait you into making a fool of yourself."

"They already had done that."

"No." Coach shook his head. "All they proved was that they were a bunch of idiots. Any gang of boys can bully somebody. They wanted you to react...to explode and make a spectacle of yourself. You didn't.

"You can hold your head up high." Coach leaned back and lit up a cigarette. "We'll get them come Monday night."

* * * *

Monday night came. Momma and I sat by the radio. I wanted so badly to go to Kossuth but couldn't get a ride. Momma said there would be plenty of other games.

That was true, along with the honest reality that Momma was trying to save her money for Christmas coming up. I didn't make a fuss.

I was in a better mood after talking with Coach Carver. Around school, everyone seemed to have heard of the incident. Coach had been right about feeling good for walking away. I would have made a spectacle of myself. Instead, I was getting pats on the back.

Larry told me not to wash my shirt and wear the orange stain like a badge of honor. He was kidding, or I think he was. For a brief moment, I thought it might be funny, but Momma would have thought I had gone plum crazy.

Momma lit a cigarette at the kitchen table when the game was about to start. She would get so nervous. It was almost like she was playing the game or something.

"Turn it up, Dean," she told me and gestured for me to move back from the radio.

Sometimes it was hard to hear on the old thing. I would hafta put my ear up to the speaker. Tonight, we were lucky. The game came in clear.

"We'll be underway momentarily with the tip-off, folks."

The voice of Happy Hal, the radio announcer for Prentiss County basketball, carried over the waves. For the next two hours, the world for the small community of New Site would center on this high school basketball game. If you weren't there at the game, you were listening to it on the radio.

"This is early in the season, but you can't tell that from the turnout to see these two undefeated teams. The Royals have traveled into Alcorn County for this showdown," Happy Hal said. "I can tell you if you have never seen the Royals play, you would think they don't have a chance. Kossuth is big and physical. The Royals are short, having only one player over six feet. But you would be making a mistake to count the Royals out. I have never seen such a well-disciplined team with one of the best coaches in the state.

"The fans tonight believe this is going to be a barn burner. It's so crowded that the boys will be barely able to pass the ball in from out of bounds."

The tip-off went to Kossuth, but from there, it was all Royals. My nerves calmed, hearing Happy Hal tell of Royal's aggressive play forcing Kossuth to turn it over and coming back down on offense.

"The Royals have spread the court. Forward Jimmy Massey passes the ball to the Royals' point guard, Troy Barnes, who stands there with the ball under his arm. The referee is counting with his fingers. Kossuth's defense comes out on Barnes. He dribbles right and hits Donnie Morris in the middle. Morris fakes right, back to the left, and lays in two. The Royals have an early lead."

Listening, I heard Happy Hal telling of how the Royals had slowed the game down.

"I'll tell you, folks, these Royals came to play. You can see the confidence. These kids know each other well, especially Morris and Barnes. Barnes has found a way to get it into his center despite Morris being guarded by Kossuth's big man, Landry. I'll tell you this Donnie Morris is as good as they come."

Though the Royals had slowed the game down, time seemed to speed by. The game was never in doubt.

"Barnes has dribbled into the corner. Time is expiring," Happy Hal said as the buzzer blew. "That's it. The Royals win forty-three to thirty-eight and stay undefeated. I have to add that Donnie Morris scored thirty-nine of the Royals points. He put on a show against Landry. There is a definite feeling of something special in the air this season for the Royals."

Chapter Six

Everywhere I went, everyone was talking about the last game played and whether the team would have enough to win State.

After the Kossuth game, Troy said that the team had shown they had what it took but cautioned, "Coach said to take one game at a time."

Which was a good thing, because the dream of going undefeated went up in smoke the next week with a loss to Neshoba County. I was happy I was listening to it on the radio and not there at the game.

We were cheated, plain and simple. Troy didn't use that excuse. He just said that they would get them next week when they came to New Site.

I couldn't wait for payback. Momma asked me why I was so upset. It was just one game and, she added, I wasn't on the team yet.

Guess that was a good point. Maybe I was using Troy's season as a diversion, so I wouldn't think so much about mine. The junior high team was doing just fine. We had only lost one game, too, but my play was off.

Troy said it was because I thought too much. I needed to just play. "There's nothing wrong with your hustle. Your shot needs to be instinct. That's all. You have the heart. Coach says that's what you need. Don't be so hard on yourself."

There was more that was bothering me than my shot. I wanted to play point. How could I get better if I wasn't getting the ball? There was nothing I could do about it. Larry played point. I was on the wing. I swallowed my frustration.

My brother had picked me up in Momma's car at school after the junior high played Thrasher. I didn't complain about the game to Troy because we won. Troy always told me that was all that mattered—if the team won.

Troy told me to cheer up, and I think I would have if I had felt like I was part of the win. Coach Douglas didn't play me but half the game. I only scored four points, though I stole the ball six times and assisted on Larry's lay-ups.

"Why don't we go to the Hobo Station and get a treat before going home?"

I smiled. Troy always thought an ice cream sandwich would solve any problem.

Troy parked in between the gray Ford truck of Mr. Lambert, who was the janitor at school, and the white and red one of Mr. Stricklen. He had a pig farm not far from here. Before we walked inside, I could hear the arguing.

"I tell you, Billy. I ain't seen nothing like it at a game. It was like we were going into battle."

"We ain't in Vietnam, Hank."

"Couldn't tell the other night…"

The voices faded when the men saw Troy. The small group sat around a checkerboard on a wooden barrel. Dressed in overalls with only one strap hooked, Mr. Green, the owner of the Hobo Station, chewed on a wad of tobacco and spit in a spittoon.

A smile broke across Old Man Stricklen's face. Leaning back in his straw-back chair, the elderly man greeted us. "Tough game against Neshoba County. I swear it was like walking in a mine field."

"Can't say it didn't feel that way," Troy said, exchanging a knowing look with me. We weren't leaving until Troy relived that night.

"Should have never gone down to Philadelphia if you ask me," Mr. Green said. "Just going down there was inviting trouble."

"What did you expect Coach Carver to do?" Mr. Stricklen began after he moved his red checker. He looked up. "That daggum coach in Tupelo won't play us."

"We don't need to go lollygagging around Mississippi to be recognized. We got all the competition right here in Prentiss county," Mr. Green muttered under his breath. "Can't say I blame Kermit Davis for not playing us. What would Tupelo gain? Nothing. If they won, they were supposed to because they're a bigger school. If they lose…"

"Don't go giving me that," Old Man Stricklen interrupted. "Ain't having it. Tupelo was just plain scared."

Mr. Green huffed. "Smart coach if you ask me. Tupelo would have had everything to lose and nothing to gain. Coach Davis was at the Kossuth game. He knows we're good."

"We needed more competition before the playoffs," Old Man Stricklen retorted.

"Don't mean that we go jumping into a lion's den," Mr. Green countered. "Not worth it. We hadn't even ran on court and Coach Carver looked like he was having a heart attack. The fans threw cups at the boys. Didn't they, Troy?"

"Yes, sir," Troy replied politely. "Never have had that happened before. Their fans were unruly."

"Heck," Mr. Lambert said. "I have never seen such heckling. It's no wonder Coach got mighty angry."

"How could you tell, Hank?" Mr. Green responded with clear sarcasm in his voice. "When Coach threw his towel on the floor or when he stomped over to the official and pulled out his ever-handy rulebook in his back pocket?"

"That official didn't care if it was a rule or not, which made Coach even angrier, and Coach ain't one to hide his feelings," Old Man Stricklen shook his head. "Just riled the crowd up more Coach pointing to the exact spot and the official paying him no mind."

Troy nodded. "Coach was trying to tell the official that the rule states that after a score, a player doesn't have to stand still to throw the ball in, but the official threatened Coach if he took another step, he would throw Coach out. The official said he could care less what the rulebook said. He knew the rules and didn't need any stupid book to tell him. Then, the official told Coach to throw his rulebook away."

Pressing his lips tightly together, Mr. Lambert shrugged, "Mighta been a good idea to have taken you guys off the court at that time."

"I'll give you that Coach's face turned beet red when the official said they made up their own rules, but in the huddle, he was calm and told us to just play our game. He would worry about the refs."

"Freddie must not have heard," Mr. Green said. "Getting the technical from the bench cost us…although the look on his face was comical."

Troy frowned. I don't think that Troy liked anyone making fun of his friend even in jest. "Don't think it was Freddie saying anything. At least he swore it wasn't to Coach."

"Don't think it would have made any difference." Old Man Stricklen's eyebrows came together. He took a deep breath. "They weren't going to let you guys win no matter what. Just a bunch of idiots."

"It wasn't just them refs," Mr. Lambert continued. "Those fans were obnoxious, especially that one directly behind the bench. That toothless drunk hounded you guys all night. *Stick your rulebook up your ass! Bunch of morons! Betcha can't tie your own sneakers!*"

"Yes, sir," Troy said. "We heard him clear enough. Most of what he was saying can't be repeated. I was glad when I heard the final buzzer. Not a moment too soon, either. It was only going to get worse. Almost did."

The incident hadn't been on the radio, but everyone was talking about it at school. Coach held it all together until the guys were going into the locker room. A coke bottle came flying out of the stands and hit Stuart in the back of the head.

"I didn't see it happen," Troy admitted. "I only saw Stuart fall down. When I looked back, Coach asked Stuart he was okay. When Stuart nodded, Coach flew into the stands. It was that same guy that was on our back all night. He scrambled out of the stands, tripping and falling. Coach leaped after him, but that guy wanted no part of Coach."

"Stuart's okay, I hope," Mr. Green said, spitting again. "That guy should have been arrested."

"Coach said that Neshoba County apologized for the incident. They said the guy has been a problem in the past, and that they were banning him from the gym," Troy said. "As for Stuart, Coach took him out to the Emergency Room at Booneville after we got back. He's fine. Lucky it wasn't more than a bump on the back of his head."

"Coach must be livid," Old Man Stricklen offered.

"About as much as you would expect," Troy said. "But we're working on a welcome when they come here next week."

* * * *

Coach Carver was mad. Sitting in the bleachers watching practice, I felt bad for my brother. Really, I felt bad for all of them.

The team had lost the night before to Kossuth at Booneville's Round Robin tournament. The regular season was coming to an end quickly.

As I had expected, the boys got their revenge on Neshoba County when they came to New Site. Between Coach Carver and Mr. Jones, they made certain there was no retribution toward Neshoba County except on the court.

It helped that Neshoba County didn't bring many fans with them. We won handily, 80-55.

The only other loss came on a road trip to Selmer, Tennessee. The team had a twenty-three and three record now, with four games to go until the playoffs.

Despite only losing by two points to Kossuth, Coach wasn't happy. The team didn't play well, and District playoffs were coming up.

Sweat poured down Troy's face as he pulled himself back to the line and waited for the whistle to blow again. Panting heavily, Donnie and Jimmy slowly got back to the line. The others followed suit along with Freddie, who seemed to be in almost a crawl.

Coach blew and released the whistle. The boys ran the final suicide, and each collapsed as they crossed the line.

"When you feel you have nothing left to give in a game, remember how you feel right now. Dig deep to give everything you have." Coach stepped down to the court and walked in front of them. "Your effort last night disappointed me, not the loss. Your mindset wasn't to win but to survive. You missed free throws, forgot to press after a score, threw the ball away, and fouled because you weren't in position. You thought they're a tough team. We beat them once so it's okay to lose.

"Never! Never step on a court unless it's to win! Your one objective is to win. You will give everything you have to accomplish that goal, or you will not play. Some nights, the ball might not fall for you no matter what you try, but there is never a night you quit and give up on a game…no matter what! Is that understood?"

I saw each player look straight at Coach. In unison, the whole team said, "Yes, sir."

Something about that moment struck a chord with me. I knew it would never leave.

* * * *

A few weeks later, I woke to the sound of the door closing. It was Saturday, but Momma was leaving for work. Getting up, I walked into the kitchen to find Troy eating a bowl of Sugar Pops dressed in an old T-shirt and shorts.

"I'm going to the gym to shoot around," Troy said in between bites.

Glancing up at the clock, I was confused. "It's three hours before practice."

"Some of the guys are going up there early."

The news wasn't surprising. District playoffs started Wednesday night.

"Can I come up after I do chores?" I asked, pulling a bowl down to join him. "I'll walk. It's a nice day."

Looking out the window, I saw the sun shining brightly in the fresh February morning air. Already, I felt the temperature rising. A draft under the kitchen door usually left the house cold, and Troy or I would turn on the stove to warm up the room until we had to leave. This morning, Troy hadn't bothered.

"Sure, why not?"

Outside, a car horn beeped. Freddie was here.

Troy got up and ruffled my hair. "See ya there."

Finishing up my breakfast, I hurried through cleaning up the dishes and feeding the animals. I checked the wire around the hen house. We had lost a couple of good hens this winter through a hole in the fence. Some varmint got in and got them.

I was on my way in less than an hour. I didn't mind walking. It was a little brisk, but I warmed up quickly. If the season was still going on for me, I probably would have run, but the junior high season had ended the previous week.

Turning onto the main road, I saw a truck driving in my direction. I recognized the blue Chevy. It was Coach.

He slowed and stopped when he saw me. Reaching over to the passenger door, he rolled down the window. "You going to the gym? I can give you a ride."

"Yeah, sure."

I opened the door and hopped inside. With a cigarette burning in his right hand, he took a puff and flicked the ashes into an overflowing ashtray. In the bed of the truck, his German Shepherd, Skippy, sat near the edge. The dog gave me a look, but nothing else.

Thank goodness. Stuart said that he thought that dog was going to eat him up once when Coach had forgotten his keys, and Stuart went back to his house to get them.

Stuart said he didn't see the dog when he knocked on the front door, but no sooner than he had, the German Shepherd came bounding from the back. Good fortune smiled on him, though. Mrs. Carver rounded the corner and called Skippy off before the dog attacked.

Coach had a pretty wife, petite with dark brown hair, and she had the sweetest smile. At the games, she always looked nervous with a cigarette in her hand. Their kids would be running around. I believe there were three of them. Momma liked her. Said she was pleasant and acknowledged her on sight.

That was important to Momma. She never said so, but I knew it bothered her that some people looked down their noses at us.

"Where's Troy?" he asked.

"Troy's already up there. He said the guys were going there to shoot, and it was ok if I went."

"Of course, it is," Coach said. "It's why I let you guys work out there at any time. I'm never gonna stop anyone from playing ball if they want. Heard you had a good year."

My ears perked up. *He thinks I had a good year!* I stumbled over my words. "Well, I got moved to wing...didn't really score that much..."

He took another puff of the cigarette. "Don't be so hard on yourself, Dean. You hustle, and you know how to play great defense. Couldn't ask for more. Looking forward to seeing what you can do in high school."

"Yes, sir. Can't wait." My voice betrayed my excitement. "I do try and hustle."

"Hustle will get you places," Coach said. "Hustle and desire."

"Is that how you got to be so good?"

He chuckled. "Don't know how good I was, but everything I did, I gave it my all."

"Mr. Jones said that you could shoot the eyes out of the basket. He called you a ball hawk."

"He did, did he? Whatever for?" Coach took another puff off his cigarette.

"Jimmy was talking to Larry and me about you working with him on his shot. Mr. Jones overheard us. He told us a lot of interesting things about when you played ball. He told us that after you played at Northeast that no major college offered you a scholarship, but you walked on at MS State. At try-outs, Coach Gregory signed you after you ended up in the fourth row of the bleachers for going after a ball out of bounds."

I didn't add that Mr. Jones bragged on him. Mr. Jones told us that how Coach's dad forbade him from playing ball, but Coach Carver made a deal with his dad to be able to play by promising to do his chores after he got home. He said that many nights Coach would be out in the barn well until after ten p.m., but he got to play ball.

"You have to play with your heart," Coach said, turning into the school's parking lot. He parked in front of the gym. I hated for the conversation to end. "Go on in and shoot around. I've got to find me some coffee."

Reaching for the door handle, I watched him grab a couple of thick folders sitting by him. I saw notes of some of the papers sticking out. *Drives to the right. Flat-footed on defense. Fakes once and then drives toward the basket.*

Getting out of the truck, I realized those were notes on other teams. I wasn't surprised. Stuart had told me that every time he stopped over at Coach's house, there were papers of scouting reports spread all over the kitchen table.

Troy was right about Coach. He didn't stop at practice. This man lived basketball.

* * * *

"Try it again, Momma," I pled, the car sputtered and stalled again. "It'll turn over."

Looking at my watch, it was almost four o'clock. We needed to leave soon if we had any chance of making it over to Delta State for Troy's next game at the North Half. Delta State was deep in the heart of the delta. We hadn't been able to make it Wednesday night when the team beat Crowder.

I had had to wait until Momma got home before leaving for the game. Thankfully, Momma didn't have to work the next morning and planned to stay over for the finals.

Missing the first game at the North Half had bothered me, but it couldn't be helped. Delta State was a little over three hours away. There was no way Momma could have gone and made it back for work.

Troy understood. "Just don't want you guys to miss the finals."

It seemed like all of our community was going to the game. Dad's family had called and said they were going.

Grandmother and Grandpa Barnes were going over to the game with Uncle Orson and Aunt Maude. Grandpa had just bought a Ford Galaxy. My cousin Rachel had told me he had sold some timber to buy the car. I'm sure he got a good deal with Uncle Orson being a car salesman.

Before they left, my uncle had called, "You're going to be late if you don't leave soon."

I wanted to tell Uncle Orson we couldn't because our car wouldn't start, but then I thought what good would it have done. It wasn't like he would have done anything to help like offer us a ride.

Momma tried it one more time. Thankfully, the car started. My heart calmed. *We will make it.*

"I have to stop at Johnson's to get it looked at."

My heart pounded again. Time was against us. No matter if they were quick, we were going to be late.

"Sorry, Dean," Momma said. "But I don't know if we will make it if I don't."

I knew she was right, but I was itching to get over to the game. Pulling into the gas station, Momma parked inside the garage. We knew the mechanic, Tommy Reed, Momma's third cousin.

I got out and got us some snacks for the drive. Fifteen. Twenty. Twenty-five minutes passed. We finally got back on the road over half-an-hour later with a car fixed: a new battery and alternator.

Momma's face dropped when Tommy handed her the bill. He saw it too.

"Don't worry about it now, Lorna," Tommy said. "Give me what you can when you can. Get on outta here and go to that game. Tell Troy we're keeping our fingers crossed."

Momma nodded, but I noticed tears welled in her eyes. As we turned back onto the highway, I reached over and patted her hand.

"Don't worry, Momma. We'll get to be there at least for the second half...and we'll be there for the game tomorrow."

She gave me a little smile and drove as fast as she could to the game. We got there when the second half began.

Walking inside the gym, she lost her smile the moment we saw the score. I had to take a second look at the scoreboard. The Royals were losing by twenty points.

Staring at the team they were playing, I shook my head. This couldn't be right. Not against this team. Yocona's uniforms were dirty. None of the team had the same sneakers, and some had holes in the bottom of their soles. Not only that, but the players also looked like they had just come in from the cotton field.

I stood on the first foot of the steps going up to our side of the bleachers and caught Troy's eyes right before tip-off. He looked relieved to see us.

Coming in late, Momma squeezed into a seat by Aunt Marilyn. I made my way over to the Royals' side, but there weren't any seats. Larry waved at me but shook his head about a seat. I had no choice but to stand to the side, which was okay with me. My nerves wouldn't let me sit.

The boys came out in a full-court press and hit Yocona hard. They began to cut into the lead.

"Boy, you were lucky you weren't here for the first half."

I turned to find Larry by my side. Figured he couldn't stand sitting either.

"We had car trouble. Can't believe this."

"It was awful. We couldn't do a thing right," Larry said. "I betcha Coach gave it to them at half."

Nodding absently, I agreed, but my attention was on the game. I held my breath on every shot and rooted for the steal. At the start of the fourth quarter, our team was only down by five. Midway through the fourth, the Royals took the lead and didn't let go of it. They roared passed Yocona, beating them sixty to fifty-four.

For a long moment, I didn't feel the pain of Larry digging his fingers into my shoulder. Then, we leaped in the air.

Racing onto the floor, I found Troy and hugged him. He broke from me. "I was worried when you guys weren't here at the beginning of the game."

"The car had trouble. We had to stop and get it looked at. It took a while." Even to myself, I sounded like I was rambling. My curiosity was on the game. "What happened to you guys?"

Troy wiped his brow. "We judged the book by its cover."

"What?"

"I've got to go and get dressed and watch the next game." He slapped my back. "I'll meet up with you in the stands."

The officials had already begun to clean the floor. Anguilla was playing Walnut Grove in fifteen minutes. The teams were waiting to take the court.

Withdrawing back to the stands, I found Momma and Grandmother. I watched the game with little interest in the teams. I had this need to make sure Troy was okay. I was worried about the expression I had seen in his eyes when he saw us walk into the gym.

The guys had dressed quickly and found a place in the crowd to sit together not far from us. All around us, I began to hear the half-time talk Coach Carver gave the team. Most of it came from Uncle Orson telling Grandpa. Listening, I knew Uncle Orson watered down the conversation because Coach's speeches weren't for mixed company.

"Coach took them to town! Blasted them out! Told them that they thought they were better than Yocona because of the way they looked. Thought that all the boys had to do was go on the court."

Looking over my shoulder, I caught Troy's eyes. A sudden realization dawned on me that my big brother's distraction may not have been that he had taken the other team for granted. I knew my brother well enough to know he wouldn't have done that. His game had been affected by our absence.

Troy was always looking after Momma and me. Boy, was I proud of him. Proud to call him my brother.

Coach Carver sat in front of his team. If he had been mad at half-time, he wasn't now. His expression showed his pride in the boys. He was laughing at something Donnie said. He was obviously relieved about beating a team that could have easily ended their season and their dreams about State.

Right before the half-time buzzer sounded, Troy slid down beside me. For the first couple of minutes, his attention was on Momma, Grandpa, and Uncle Orson. Then, he nudged into me.

"Glad you saw the good part of the game," Troy said. "It was bad. Thought we were done for...but it was Coach that brought us back."

"I heard he reamed you guys out." I stared at Coach while I talked. He was writing down notes.

"Yeah, he did, for not playing with our hearts like Yocona was, but it was more." Troy pressed his lips together tightly. "He told us that a twenty-point deficit is hard to make up, but not impossible. Everything we had worked for all year was on the line...all the hard practices...the running.

"He reminded us of our mission and told us it does not end here. Then, he proceeded to tell us how to beat them with the press. Told us not to look at the score, but to play...and not to quit." Troy paused for a moment and then repeated. "He said not to quit. We didn't."

* * * *

What a run.

The next night, I watched the Royals win the North Half Tournament against Anguilla. With the top three teams advancing, the excitement continued to the State

Tournament. Luckily, State was played at New Albany, which was less than an hour from New Site.

There would be no problem driving back and forth to the games. I wouldn't have to miss a game.

We would be playing Yocona, who had made it to State as the number three seed again after beating New Augusta. This time, Yocona didn't stand a chance. The Royals were focused and determined.

Coach Carver's team was on the brink of winning their first Class B championship. We were in the finals, and I had never seen Troy happier. The entire school was in high spirits, and Troy was ecstatic.

It was like the best Christmas ever…in March.

Most of all our family had come over at one time or another after the North Half win. Troy had sat on the porch and recounted the games at least a dozen times. Each time the story got more exaggerated, and Troy enjoyed every minute of it.

I saw the pride in Momma's eyes. She was in a different mood. Not once during the week had she mentioned money, not even the cost of fixing the car. Though, I suspected some of it was the fact that Grandma Taylor had asked if we wanted to come live with her.

We were going to be moving about a mile down the road into a four-bedroom bricked ranch with indoor plumbing. My Great-Aunt Ruth was going to live with her daughter in Alabama. Her daughter needed help with her children. Since Grandma Taylor couldn't live independently because of her diabetes, Aunt Ruth said we could live with Grandma. The move would happen after Troy's season ended.

Troy walked around with a permanent smile on his face. A little cocky, too, I might add. While I was helping Momma pack, he was *resting* and would sit around watching TV. I don't think he ever missed an episode of Gunsmoke or Bonanza.

Momma wouldn't dare fuss at Troy. He had an important game to prepare for and needed to concentrate on it. There would be no distractions for her boy.

I supposed there was some sound reasoning behind Momma letting Troy laze around, for he was playing the best ball I had seen him play. On the other hand, I had already moved the chickens up to Grandma Taylor's chicken coop.

Lucky for me, there was less than a week after North Half until the State Tournament. I swallowed my growing frustration toward my brother's expectations of being waited on like some kind of prince.

Yet, I almost lost it when Troy threw his laundry at me to wash before he left for State. I threw it back.

"Do it yourself."

"Ah, come on," Troy said. "The guys want to shoot around, and I have nothing clean. I'll do it for you when you go to State."

"You won't even be around then," I shot back. "I don't have anyone to boss around."

Troy smiled. "I promise, no matter where I'm at, I will come back and be your lackey."

I laughed. I couldn't help it. Troy left knowing he would have clean clothes for the tournament.

The finals for the Royals started late Saturday night, coming after the early afternoon semi-finals. The team took on Puckett, the number one seed from the South.

I got there early and managed to get a seat directly behind our bench beside Larry. The rest of the junior high team sat around us.

The gym was packed. I didn't think they could squeeze another person in, but fans kept pouring inside on both sides.

Momma nervously sat up in the bleachers beside Aunt Marilyn and Grandma Barnes. She wasn't the only one anxious. Coach Carver's wife sat directly down from Momma, smoking one cigarette after another.

The guys and I paid little attention to the consolation game. We came alive when it came time for our team to take the floor. My attention was drawn to the players as they warmed up. I could only imagine what they were feeling. My body tingled with the thought that maybe one day I could be there like Troy.

With the title at stake, both teams came ready to play. Our cheers escalated on tip-off. Bucket for bucket, the game soon became apparent that the teams were evenly matched.

The first half was quickly coming to a close. Puckett drove to the basket. Donnie stepped in front of his opponent, hoping for an offensive foul. Instead, Donnie was charged with the foul. Puckett's center stepped to the line and hit both, tying the score at thirty-two.

Donnie frowned as he made his way down the court. Seconds ticked off to the half, 10—9—8. Glenn threw the ball into Troy, who dribbled over the half-court line. He made a lob pass to Donnie, who was running toward the basket. Donnie tossed in an easy lay-up with only one dribble, giving the Royals a two-point lead at the half.

The third period was all Royals. I found myself able to breathe, because the spark from the close of the half had continued. At the end of the third quarter, we were up by six. Watching our team huddle between periods, I heard Coach Carver say, "We have to finish. Don't let up. They're not done. They are too good a team."

Coach was right. Puckett dug into the lead. I saw Coach slap the court with his towel. He pointed to Troy, who nodded.

The look Troy gave Coach left no doubt in my mind that we were going to win. There was no panic in his eyes, only confidence. Time and time again, Troy dished the ball around, but mostly to Donnie. No matter who Troy passed it to, they hit one bucket after another.

Coach Carver called a time-out with a minute to go and a four-point lead. I couldn't make out what was said this time, but I saw Troy nod in unison with the others. The huddle broke. The pressure mounted with time running down.

They couldn't make a mistake. They didn't.

The game was tight all the way, but when the final buzzer rang, the Royals had secured the first Class B State Championship in Mississippi.

Chapter Seven

The entire community celebrated the championship. Prentiss County was basketball country.

"We know what it takes to win," Troy said. "We might battle hard during the season but respect each other."

The morning after winning State, the team returned triumphant. A celebratory parade greeted the Royals in Frankstown. Booneville's Mayor Smith, along with Booneville's police cars and Royals fans, lined up to escort the team to one of the town's favorite restaurants, Jack Sprat's.

Beaming with pride, Momma was so happy. Troy was named All-State, along with Donnie and Barry.

Troy's team had only one more hurdle to face—the Grand Slam.

This was the first year that there was going to be four teams playing for the overall title. Usually, there were only two fighting for the crown.

Momma got to go, but I stayed with Grandma Taylor and listened to it on the radio. The game was held all the way down in Jackson, over four hours away.

Logically, I understood the odds weren't great. I mean, we were a small school going against teams with much larger enrollment. At least, Pelahatchie was BB, so I thought we had a chance. Listening on the radio, I held onto hope going into the fourth quarter with the score tied, but Pelahatchie pulled away after that.

The loss didn't take away from the State title for me. I considered the Grand Slam an impossible dream. We had won our championship.

Troy said he hoped this feeling of being champs wouldn't fade.

Can't say that it did.

The celebration continued with Troy's graduation.

High school graduation was a big thing around New Site. Announcements had gone out, and Troy was reaping the benefits.

Day after day, I fetched handfuls of cards from our mailbox, all addressed to Troy.

The Saturday before graduation, Troy sat at the breakfast table, shuffling through a pile of cards from well-wishers. "I think more people remembered my graduating than I sent announcements."

I shrugged, feeling a tad jealous…okay, maybe a little more than a tad. "I reckon I wouldn't know."

Making my way into the kitchen, I grabbed a Coke and started looking through the cabinet for a snack. I didn't find much more than some stale crackers.

"Look in the top cabinet," Troy said from behind me. "That's where Grandma keeps the Moon Pies."

Grandma shouldn't have had any sweets in the house, not with her diabetes. At least, that's what I told myself when I grabbed a banana one for me and a vanilla for Troy. I threw it over to him.

"Thanks." Troy tore open the sweet. "I have the keys to the gym. Want to come with me?"

"Why not?" I said after I took a bite. "I don't have anything else planned."

I had to admit living with Grandma was turning out just fine. The house was nice enough and big enough for us, and it had indoor plumbing. Not to mention, Grandma was a great cook. I loved her fried green tomatoes, biscuits, and gravy.

Most days, Troy had friends over. Grandma didn't mind and seemed to enjoy the company. She would sit out on the porch and play checkers with anyone who took the challenge. Grandma was awfully good. I knew I would lose eight out of ten times. When the guys came over, most of them were good sports and played her, knowing they were bound to lose.

Grandma was taking her afternoon nap when we left for the gym. We took her car, which had kinda become Troy's. She let him take it anywhere he wanted. Troy enjoyed it. Especially since he started bringing his girlfriend over to the house.

I supposed when it came to girls, Missy White was nice enough. Pretty, with shoulder-length brown hair, she lived in Marietta. Her daddy owned a garage outside of Booneville. That was where Troy met her. He had taken Momma's car in to get fixed.

The problem I had with her was that she was over all the time. The last few months, it had been Missy, Missy, Missy. I would turn around, and she would be underfoot, smiling, and giggling at anything Troy did.

The day was hot, not much different than any other day lately. I took a jug of water because I knew we would be at the gym for a while.

Coach never denied any of his boys the keys to the gym when they asked, not even those who were graduating. Coach was like that.

When we got there, I was a little surprised. No one else was there, just us two. Usually, there were at least three or four guys shooting around.

"You didn't call anyone else?"

Troy grinned. "Nope. I wanted it to be just the two of us…like we used to do."

I smiled at the remembrance. It was like old times in the back yard with a ball.

My brother unlocked the door, and we eased inside. The empty gym seemed strange. Only a couple of months ago, scores of people crowded inside to see the Royals play ball. Now, it was quiet.

I walked to the center of the court with one thought— next year would be my turn. In my imagination I saw myself dribbling up for a jump shot. Going through the motions, I jumped, carried my arm up, and shot.

"Need to pop your wrist straight down, Dean." Troy came out of the locker room with the ball cart and bounced- passed a ball to me. "Coach will work on it with you."

Taking the ball, I shot it for real. This time I popped my wrist. Swish!

I turned to Troy with what I'm sure appeared to be a wacky grin. I said, "That's how it's done!"

Troy gave me a small clap. "Let's play twenty-one."

For the next fifteen minutes, we shot. Surprisingly, I smoked him. He couldn't buy a free throw. Sinking the last shot, I looked back at my brother.

He stood just staring at me. "You're going to be just fine."

"What are you talking about?"

"I signed up for the Air Force. I leave next month."

The words echoed in the empty gym. I shook my head.

"Come on, bro. Stop kidding. You're going to Northeast this fall."

"They didn't offer me a scholarship." Troy shrugged. "I thought I had a good tryout, but Coach Lawrence only needed one guard. He took Redman from Thrasher."

I had a sudden sinking feeling in the pit of my stomach. There was a war going on— Vietnam.

Grandma watched the news every night. All I could see in my mind was the killing and continuous bombing.

"Why?" I finally managed to question. Then a fit of sudden anger replaced my shock. I threw the ball as hard as

I could at Troy. "Why would you do that to Momma…to me? You weren't drafted."

Blocking the ball, Troy let it dribble to a stop. He frowned.

"Don'tcha think I thought about that?" he said. "Lots of us are doing it. Why Sander's oldest is in the army over there."

"But you didn't have to," I countered. "You're deserting us."

His eyes blazed as he rushed at me and yanked me up by my T-shirt. "Don't you ever say that? Do you understand?"

He slung me down hard on the court.

"What else do you want me to do? Stay home and become Dad? A no-good drunk." He pressed his lips tight together. "I want more, Dean. I have a plan. Serve my country, come home, and go to college. It will get me the GI bill so I can. I'm going to make something of myself."

Crawling back to my feet, I sucked in a deep breath. His leaving terrified me more than I wanted to admit. Glancing over at him, I saw there would be no talking him out of it. Once he made up his mind, there was no changing it.

He walked over to me. "Look, I need you to be okay with this. Momma will need you…"

"I need you," I admitted my own selfishness. "I can't do this without you."

He gave me a light punch on my shoulder. "You're wrong, little brother. You've been looking after Momma for a while. Now… I feel comfortable leaving. You guys will be fine living with Grandma…and I'm going to be sending money home every month."

Mortified, I found tears welling in my eyes. As I wiped them back, I was glad Troy didn't make fun of me.

"Besides, you don't think I'm not going to be bragging about my brother," he said. "You're going to be on the best basketball team in the state. The things you're going to achieve! I see it now." Overexaggerating, he waved his arm toward the stands. "And the fans go wild!"

I did the only thing I could do. I got up and picked up a ball.

"I don't want to talk anymore. Let's play."

Alleviating both our frustrations, we played hard. I had grown over Troy a few inches and found that I had begun to win a few one-on-one games. That or Troy let me win...which wasn't a possibility. Troy hated losing.

Less than and an hour later, some of the guys showed up.

Troy laughed. "It never fails. Open the gym, and everyone shows up."

* * * *

Graduation came and went.

Momma had been in her glory when Troy walked up to get his diploma. She had gone and bought a new dress, pale blue with a belt at the waist, and had her hair done and pretty. She sat there so proud.

Grandma and I sat next to her. She clapped hard when Troy's name was called. As he walked in procession, she squeezed my hand real tight.

I had thought Momma was going to be a basket case with Troy leaving for the Air Force, but I was wrong. Momma calmed me down about Troy leaving.

"You can't be selfish, Dean. We have to let him go," she said. "Don't ya go and try and make him feel guilty neither. He's right. We're going to be just fine. He's doing something fine and good and not trying to take shortcuts like his daddy. Troy knows nothing good comes easy. He's going to make a good man. You just have to have faith and hold to it."

She seemed confident that in God's goodness, God would protect Troy. It was just like Momma to draw on her faith. I reckoned that was what she lived on while we were growing up.

Nobody else seemed upset with Troy going into the Air Force, except for Missy. She didn't cry in front of Troy, but I saw tears fall when he wasn't looking. It made me feel for her.

I guess it was something we had in common. We both were going to miss him.

Troy was right. Most people who heard about him signing up for the military didn't think it was a big deal. It was kinda expected the way they saw it. A lot of guys had done the same. God, family, and country. It was how we lived around there.

For me, though, my brother's leaving came as a harsh life lesson—nothing stays the same.

School was out. This summer, I had a job. A few of the basketball boys were helping Coach Carver build his barn.

Jimmy was picking Larry and me up early. Dressed, with my lunch ready in a brown paper bag, I was on the porch by six-thirty. We liked to go to Hunkapellar's to get breakfast before work.

I finished my biscuit long before we got to the barn. Coach had bought the land to put cattle on it. He had already fenced it in and had Charolais cattle. I had never seen them around here, solid white, and they were the meanest cows I had ever encountered.

I discovered Coach liked to be different.

The pasture was large with woods on either side. From what I saw, there was a small pond not far from the site Coach was building the barn.

The place was about half done when I started to help. I was glad I wasn't around when they put up the poles. I didn't have a problem with banging a hammer or cutting a two by four.

There were five of us basketball boys helping. Larry and I were going to be freshmen. Then there were Barry,

Jimmy, and Earl, who were coming back from last year. Two more guys from school were here as well, Ricky Cain and Travis Goddard. Coach called them his outlaws because they were in trouble all the time at school for one thing or another, but they didn't give Coach any trouble.

I knew most of the guys through Troy and basketball. I didn't really know Ricky and Travis, but I found them to be funny. They talked more than they worked, but they always had us laughing.

This morning, Jimmy and I took to the roof alongside Coach to nail down the tin because we weren't afraid of heights. The day promised to be a hot one. We needed to do what we could before the sun got too high and made it too hot to work.

With a nail in my mouth, I looked up to see Ricky and Travis driving up. They were late as usual. Larry had already started moving some wood from the back of Coach's truck to the ground.

Ricky sauntered up with Travis beside him and jokingly and punched his buddy in his shoulder. Travis pushed back. I don't think Coach was too happy with either of them.

Coach walked over to the edge of the roof and pointed to Ricky. "Hand me another piece of tin, Ricky."

I went back to my work, concentrating on banging the nail into a two by four. If I didn't keep my eye on my work, I would miss the wood, and the tin would fly back at me.

Suddenly, a scream broke the morning silence. Really it sounded more like a screech, followed by a clang.

Ricky had dropped the tin and looked like he was running for his life. Ricky was a pretty big guy, probably six-three, two-forty. I don't think he had ever run in his life, but he crossed the pasture in ten seconds flat.

"Snake! Snake!"

Coach had already jumped down, picked up a shovel, and cut the snake's head off in one swift motion. His dog,

Skippy, had leaped off Coach's truck and was barking madly at the copperhead. The large triangle head was a dead giveaway.

Jimmy and I burst into laughter. Ricky had tripped over his own feet by that time. I looked over at Coach, who stood there with a broad grin on his face.

Coach walked over to the fence and pitched the snake in the ditch. "Let's get back to work."

We ribbed Ricky for the rest of the morning. Though if the truth be known, I think if it had been me, I would have been down at the cross-road before anyone could have stopped me.

Jimmy, Larry, and I ate our lunch under a large oak and waited for everyone else to return. Coach went home for his, and the rest had gone to the store to get some more drinks.

"Did Travis ask you to go over to his house after we get off today with him and Ricky?" Larry asked, taking a bite of his peanut butter and jelly sandwich. "Just to hang out for a couple of hours."

I almost choked. Not that I didn't like either one of them, I did. They seemed cool, but everyone knew the two were notorious for driving over to Baldwyn and getting beer. We couldn't do that…could we?

"You goof. They're messing with you." Jimmy laughed, shaking his head. "Coach calls them his outlaws for a reason."

Troy always said I was too gullible. Reckoned I was, but it seemed Larry wasn't much different. I was determined not to let either of them know how naïve I was.

Joining in with Jimmy, I said, "Sometimes I worry about you, Larry."

Larry took the ribbing in his good nature spirit. "Stupid, huh? Coach would have my head."

Grinning broadly like I had realized that from the beginning, I nodded. One thing was for certain, I didn't want to get on Coach's bad side.

* * * *

"Troy, get out of the bathroom!" I knocked continually on the door. "Come on! You've been in there an hour. I gotta go."

My brother opened the door. His hair slicked back, clean shaven, and he smelled like Old Spice. He wore a new button-down, mustard-colored with grey stripes. I had to admit he looked sharp.

I let out a long whistle. "Missy is a lucky girl."

"You think?" Troy asked.

At first, I didn't think he was serious. Troy had always carried himself with confidence I wished I had. This evening, something was different. He was nervous.

Troy was leaving on Monday. Momma was fixing a special dinner for him tomorrow night and having the whole family over. Tonight, he was taking his girl out for their last date before they parted ways for a long time.

"Yeah, you look great," I said, pushing by him. "Now, get out of my way."

Shutting the bathroom door, I heard him say goodbye to Momma and Grandma.

"Going to be a little late tonight," he said. "I'm taking Missy down to Tupelo. Don't wait up."

He was long gone by the time I walked back into the living room. I let out a long sigh. Grandma had set herself in front of the TV to watch Lawrence Welk. It was going to be a struggle to get her to switch to Gomer Pyle.

"I think this is a repeat, Grandma," I began. A quick glance over at Momma told me I wasn't gonna get my way on this one. She raised her eyebrows in a way that told me to sit down.

I wasn't in the mood to argue. Too tired. After making some Jiffy-Pop popcorn, I sat down on the couch. While reading the latest edition of Good Housekeeping, Momma reached over and took a handful.

Thankfully, when Lawrence Welk finished, Grandma went to bed. Momma didn't care if I watched Gunsmoke.

A knock on the door disturbed the opening credits. I looked over at Momma. We never had visitors at this time of night. I got up on the second knock.

Opening the door, Brother Bennett stood on the porch. My heart caught in my throat before he uttered a word. I knew immediately something was wrong—bad wrong. It was in his eyes.

"Get your mother, son. We need to get to the hospital," he said as he gestured with his arm toward his car. "Troy has been in an accident."

* * * *

I don't remember much about the drive into Booneville, except there was a deathly silence in the car. Momma stared out the window with an empty look on her face.

The emergency room was packed. Looking around, I recognized most of Troy's friends, teammates, and Coach Carver. I heard wailing and cries.

As if in a trance, I walked inside. Immediately, Momma was greeted by a doctor who took her back with Brother Bennett. I stood alone.

Suddenly, I felt a hand in mine. Turning, I saw Missy. Her eyes were smeared with mascara, and her dress was covered in blood.

"It's my fault...all my fault." Her voice faltered. "Oh, Dean, he was so still...and his eyes..."

How we got to a set of chairs, I don't know, but we sat. I hugged her like if I did, nothing bad would happen to my brother.

"Tonight wasn't supposed to end like this...we were going to Tupelo," she whispered.

"What happened?" I managed.

"Troy came to pick me up…he looked so handsome." Her voice had a faraway distant tone. "I was so excited…but Stephanie had shown up at home a few minutes before Troy got there. It didn't take long for Wade to show up. They were fighting. Daddy got in the middle of it. There was a lot of shouting."

I made no attempt to stop her story, but I didn't understand what her sister and her husband had to do with it. I wanted to know what happened to my brother.

"Troy was on the porch when Stephanie came bolting out, got in her car, and took off. Wade took off after her. I was scared…so scared for my sister 'cause Wade's got a bad temper. Daddy was getting his shotgun…I grabbed Troy's arm and pleaded with him to follow them before Daddy got hold of Wade.

"He didn't hesitate. I climbed in beside him. On the turn onto the highway, we saw Wade's truck parked…I didn't see at first…," she paused for a moment. Her hands shook uncontrollably. "Until we got out…Stephanie's car flipped at the bottom of the canal's ravine. Troy and I raced down the embankment." She gulped to catch her breath. "I couldn't believe it! Stephanie was trapped under the car…face down. Wade had already got to her side, trying to get her out. It's all a blur…Everything happened so quickly. Daddy showed up, and our neighbor, Waylon Humphries. I heard screams to get her out and lift the car. I saw Daddy drag her out from underneath the car…except…except Troy lost his footing. The ground was wet, and when the car was lifted, my attention was on Stephanie. I didn't notice Troy had fallen underneath it…"

Time seemed endless sitting there waiting for Momma to return…waiting for word on my brother. I had found a seat by myself. I didn't want to be around anyone.

Then, I heard a long wail.

My heart stopped. I was afraid to breathe.

From the corner of my eye, I saw Coach Carver walking toward me. I had a sudden urge to get out of there. The look on Coach's face scared me.

"Dean, I'm sorry."

Coach didn't say anything else. He didn't have to. I knew.

Troy was dead.

Chapter Eight

Grown men cried.

I had no tears left to cry at the funeral. I felt nothing but a growing rage that Troy was gone. *Why did he have to be a hero?*

This couldn't have happened. It is only a terrible nightmare. I just needed to wake up.

I didn't.

My reality had become a world without my brother.

The truth was I didn't remember the days after Troy's death. I survived because I realized I was still breathing, but a piece of my soul was buried with Troy that day as the rains poured.

The doctor came and gave Momma something to sleep. I don't think she ever wanted to get up. She wouldn't let me in to see her. She didn't want to see anyone.

Grandma went in despite Momma telling her not to bother her. I stood outside the door and heard them cry together.

But no amount of crying, praying, or grieving was gonna bring my brother back.

His teammates, most of whom served as pallbearers, came and offered to help in any way possible—the same with the church. I reckoned every one of them made their way through our house, with condolences and food.

Politely, I refused. The only thing I wanted, they couldn't give—I wanted my brother back.

Coach Carver came over most days. He didn't say much. We would just sit on the porch and play checkers.

"Whenever you're ready, you can start back and help with the barn," Coach said three weeks after the accident. "The boys keep asking where you are."

Making a move with my red checker, I shrugged. "Been meaning to talk to you about that. Don't think I'm coming back. Momma needs me here."

Coach didn't respond. I felt him staring at me. Looking up, I saw him frowning.

"What?" I said defensively. "I can't leave Momma."

Before I uttered the words, I knew it sounded stupid. Momma had already gone back to work. I was spending my days in front of the TV with Grandma.

"It's okay to live, Dean. The boys say you haven't even gone to the gym to shoot around."

I don't know why the words stung, but they cut deep.

"Who are you to tell me what to do?"

"Didn't mean anything by it," Coach said. "I'm just worried about you. That's all. I know you're hurting."

"You don't know what I'm feeling. How could you?" I snapped. "I'm done with it all. How's that?"

Coach pressed his lips together as if thinking about what to say but said nothing. He just sat there looking at me.

I got mad, so angry. My temper fired. I knocked the checkerboard off the wooden barrel and went into the house, slamming the door behind me. I don't know how long it took, but Coach left, leaving me alone.

* * * *

By the summer's end, visitors had trickled down to almost none. When someone showed up, I never answered the knock, nor did I answer the phone. It would make Grandma so mad at me.

Grandma got even madder when Jimmy drove up one day and wanted to talk with me. I imagined Coach had sent him.

"Don't suppose Dean is around?" I heard Jimmy ask Grandma from my bedroom window.

"Afraid not," Grandma answered. "You want me to tell him anything?"

"Yeah, if you can, ma'am. Tell him that we're shooting around one tomorrow if he wants to join us. I can come by and pick him up if he needs a ride. Won't be no problem at all. Been missing him. We're hoping that with school starting back, he'll be back soon enough."

"I'll tell him."

There was an awkward silence. After I heard the car drive off, I walked back into the living room.

"Ain't gonna do that again, Dean," she said. "It ain't right to lie to your friends. They're good boys, and maybe it's time to go back to normal living. It's been hard on us all."

I stared at Grandma for a moment. She meant well; I knew that. She was just at a loss on how to fix me.

"Yeah, sure."

I plopped back on the couch. Concentration was on TV. From the corner of my eye, I saw her shake her head. Didn't take much to figure out I was a disappointment.

Since Troy had died, I hadn't wanted to do much. I got up late and laid around the house all day. Momma kept yelling at me for one thing or another. It didn't matter the reason; I wasn't going to make her happy no matter what I did.

When she got home from work that afternoon, it was no different. She lit into me the moment she walked into the door and didn't stop. I ignored her mostly, but for some unknown reason, she walked into my room.

"Dean Michael, all your clothes are on the floor. I thought I told you to get everything set for Monday. You're starting high school."

Jumping off the couch, I ran down the hall. I didn't want her in there. "I'm fine," I said in the doorway. "I got a shirt picked out."

Momma was having none of it. She threw the jeans she had in her hand back on the floor. "Look at this mess. Get in here now and clean it up."

"Calm down." I shrugged her off. "I'll pick it up tomorrow."

"I didn't say tomorrow." Her voice escalated with every word. "I said today…now…and where are your new clothes for school? Didn't I give you money to buy some?"

I wanted to say she could have gone out and got me clothes like she used to before Troy died. Instead, I stepped inside and pulled open the top drawer of my dresser. Reaching inside, I took out a wad of cash and threw it on the bed.

"It's all there. Just haven't had any time to go get anything."

"Time?" she yelled at me. "That's all you've had. Lazy good-for-nothing. I can't believe a son of mine…" She paused and stared hard at me. "Would become such a worthless sack of shit."

"Not like Troy, huh, Momma? Maybe it should have been me that died. Would that have made you happy?"

"Maybe."

Her words hung in the air. For a long moment, all I could do was breathe, hoping she would say she didn't mean it. It didn't happen.

Turning on my heel, I ran out of the room and grabbed Grandma's keys. Behind me, I heard Grandma call out, but I didn't stop.

I got in the car and drove.

* * * *

Driving around aimlessly, I didn't have a destination. Didn't care. There was nowhere I wanted to go, only a desire to be as far away from home—Momma, Grandma, and Troy's ghost that lingered around us.

I don't know how I got there, but I saw Ricky Cain's house when I took a turn. Wasn't hard to miss. There were always a million cars parked in the front yard with a ton of random hubcaps lined up on the porch side.

A bunch of guys sat outside under a shade tree on some old metal lawn chairs that needed to be painted. I recognized Ricky and Travis and turned into the driveway. Parking, I walked over the mostly dirt lawn.

Ricky looked shocked to see me but welcomed me anyway.

"Well, look who's here. Come on, man, and pull up a chair. Want a beer?"

"Why not?" I took a seat next to Travis.

Finishing my fourth beer, I stumbled up from my chair and fell into the guy next to me. I didn't know who he was. Didn't really care.

He did. He pushed me back hard, and I ended up on the ground. Crawling to my feet, I pointed at him. "Not nice, man. Just getting another beer."

I started toward the cooler. The guy blocked my way.

"They're my beers," he said. "You ain't getting any more for free. You need to go buy some."

"Okay, okay." I nodded, holding my arm up high in the air. "I'll go. Who's coming…because." I giggled. "I don't know where I'm going."

I snorted.

"Who let this moron come?"

I turned back around to the guy who pushed me. Losing my balance, I fell. The guy howled in laughter.

Pushing myself back on my feet, I stared at the guy. My good mood was lost, replaced with a wave of sudden anger. I lunged at him and knocked him to the ground. Not letting up, I pounced on top of him.

Near as I could tell, I was about half the size of the guy. It didn't matter. I started pounding him with my fist—one right after another. I felt strong arms grab me, but I wasn't finished. I swung wildly.

Finally, someone pulled me off and held my arms back. The guy I fought got up and punched me hard in the stomach. Falling forward, I threw up.

Behind me, I heard voices. "Come on, Calvin. Dontcha know who he is? Troy's little brother."

It only made me angrier. I didn't want their pity. I didn't want anyone's pity. I would take them all on. Rearing back to swing again, I saw something through my blurred vision. Everyone seemed to have moved back, kinda like I imagine the Red Sea parting.

A man walked toward me. Coach?

It was the last thing I remember.

* * * *

The next day was a fog. My head pounded, and the whole room spun if I lifted my head. Sometimes I had to move, like when I was throwing up.

If I expected any sympathy, I was sadly disappointed. Grandma left a couple of aspirins by my nightstand with a glass of water. Momma didn't come in to check on me.

By early evening, I began to feel a little better. Coming out of the bathroom, I heard Grandma arguing with Momma about bringing me in some supper.

"If he wants anything," Momma said, "he can come out and fix it. Should take him by his ear into church in the morning."

"You know that Coach wants Dean to go with him in the morning. He asked me when he dropped him off," Grandma said. "Coach was nice enough to see after him…and saw that the boys brought back my car."

Doggoneit! It *was* Coach I had seen…and he was coming back in the morning? Oh, I felt sick again.

The next morning, I watched the sunrise from the porch. I hadn't slept all night. Grandma told me that Coach was coming by to pick me up early. Figured I owed him as much, but I had done decided I was giving up ball. I couldn't even imagine going into the gym to play a game.

It would be hard enough to go to school the following day. If I had a choice, I didn't think I would go back. Mack Johnson quit after eighth grade and was now working at Hodges Lumber Mill.

But Momma was already real mad at me. I couldn't find it in me to hurt her more. At least, I made up my mind to try to go back to school.

I saw Coach's truck driving up to the house and panicked. All the courage I had mustered up to go with Coach vanished. The speech I had come up with on why I couldn't play anymore was forgotten. I couldn't go through with telling him I wasn't going to play.

I couldn't face the man and see the disappointment in his eyes.

Jumping up, I rushed back to the front door, but it was too late. Coach had parked.

Rolling down his window, Coach said in a firm voice, "Get in."

There was one thing that hadn't changed. Wasn't gonna go against Coach. I rounded the Chevy and took a seat like I was told but clung to the door handle. I don't know what I was thinking. I certainly wasn't going to open the door and jump out. I just didn't want to be there.

Turning back on the highway, Coach went left. The way to the gym was to the right.

"Where are we going?"

"Check on some spots for hunting," Coach said. "Out behind where I'm building my house. My brothers and I have been working on the fields for dove season. Officially, it doesn't start til next week, but I thought it wouldn't hurt to scout around for the best spot. Have you ever been dove hunting?"

I shook my head. My first thought was that this wasn't going the way I thought. He caught me off-guard.

Glancing over my shoulder, I saw Skippy in the truck's bed, hanging his head out over the edge. The large German Shepherd seemed to be enjoying the ride without a worry in the world.

I had forgotten what that felt like.

Nothing else was said until we pulled onto a gravel work road by an old abandoned house and rode down to fields that had been freshly overturned.

"We're going to put some seed out." Coach gave me a knowing smile.

No one was supposed to bait fields, but everyone did it. Dove season was really big around here. I just never had the opportunity to go. I had wanted to, though. Hunting birds was different than hunting squirrels or coons.

The road was bumpy. Almost hit my head once. I was glad when we stopped.

Coach got out and took his double-barrel 12-gauge shotgun out of the gun rack. Slowly, I made my way around the truck. Skippy sat in the back, unmoving, waiting for Coach to call him.

Putting two shells into the chamber, Coach loaded his gun. He checked his vest to ensure he had enough cartridges.

Coach didn't call Skippy but pointed to the back of the truck. "There's a pair of boots you can put on and grab one of the sacks of seed."

Looking in the truck's bed, I saw what Coach was talking about...right by Skippy. For a long moment, I stared at the dog. He seemed friendly enough right now, but when I reached in, would he bite me?

I thought for a moment—the dog or Coach?

I grabbed a sack and boots. By the time I exchanged footwear, Coach was already in the middle of the field. Hustling, I threw the bag over my shoulder and caught up with him. We walked.

The morning promised a sunny day. It was already hot, but we had a nice breeze. There was a peaceful calm I hadn't felt in a long time. I had to admit something felt right, out here in the middle of nowhere.

After we threw out the seed, a small flock of doves circled overhead. Coach gestured for me to stay behind him and readied his gun on his shoulder. We stood in silence and watched the birds. I glanced over at Coach. His face tensed in concentration.

As the doves came in for a landing, Coach fired twice and killed two birds. Coach was a real good shot. Doves were fast and quick and challenging to shoot.

We walked over to where the birds fell. He picked one up and turned back to me.

"You eat dove?"

"Don't think I've had any, but Momma was just talking about them last week. She loves 'em."

"We'll get enough for y'all," he said as he reloaded the gun. "Next week, this field will be covered with hunters. One of my favorite times of the year." He pointed over to his right. I saw a tin roof reflecting the sun across the field on the other side of the barbed-wire fence. I figured it must be a shed. "After we're done with the day's hunt, we have a big cookout over there at John Dale's. He's my cousin and helps me drive the boys around during the playoffs and scouts for me, too. Troy may have mentioned him. The cookout is just us guys to hang out. Always cook up something we've never tried before. Last year, it was beaver. Do you want to shoot?"

"I haven't shot much lately… I'm not a great shot."

"Then I'll teach you."

Listening to his instructions made me feel like I did know what I was doing. When we were done, there were six birds in the bag. I had only killed one, but somehow, I felt a sense of accomplishment. I figured I would fix them up for dinner that night.

Back at the truck, Coach sat on the tailgate. My mood changed quick enough as I met his eyes.

"You're lucky you weren't beaten to a pulp," he began.

Figuring this would go quicker if I just agreed with everything he said, I said, "Yeah, I reckon."

"You're pushing everyone away."

I shrugged. What did he know about how my life fell apart? People think they know how you feel, but they don't. Yet, it doesn't stop them from telling you how you are supposed to feel. Brother Bennett kept repeating that it was God's will…that my faith will guide me through. Trust in the Lord.

Looking back across the field, I just wanted to go home, back to my room, and shut the door. I was too tired to deal with this.

"It hurts, Dean," Coach pressed. "and it's not going to change anytime soon."

I snapped my head back. I wanted to yell at him, but he was Coach. All I could do was stare at him.

"You just have to keep on living until the pain lessens…when you can remember Troy as the man he was. You think now that day will never come. You're mad at him for leaving you, but one day it will hit you how lucky you were to have had him in your life. I know I was. Troy was a special person."

"You don't have to tell me! I know! I know!" Suddenly, I lost control and screamed. "He was my brother…He wasn't supposed to die. He promised…promised me he would watch *me* play ball. He left me…"

I fell to my knees and cried into my hands. I hadn't cried since before the funeral.

Coach moved over to my side. "I'm sorry, son."

Shaking my head, I wiped back my tears. Choking on my words, I admitted, "It's not just Troy I'm mad at... I'm mad at everyone... Momma...Missy...I'm mad at God."

The words hung in the air. I couldn't look at Coach in the eyes. He had to think I was the devil incarnate.

"I understand."

I shook my head. I didn't believe he could have been mad at God. Not Coach. He must have seen my disbelief.

"How could there be a God that would allow Troy to die? You have begun to doubt God's very existence," Coach continued. "I think that's natural to question when you're hurting."

As he talked, I began to understand that Coach knew the pain I was going through. I felt the tension leave my body. I stood up, and Coach took a step back.

"I don't have all the answers and don't understand why God lets bad things happen to good people. We just have to hold to faith that one day we'll find out," Coach said solemnly. He took a deep breath. "There are no written rules on how to grieve, Dean. There's no timetable on when it's supposed to stop hurting, and sometimes a wave of pain will overwhelm you even years later."

"Then, how am I going to go on without him...?" Again, I found myself choking up. "I don't understand why...why Troy?"

"Son, I wish I had an answer for you. All I can tell you is that's the way life is. But it's what we do with our life that matters. I have always felt we all have a purpose, and when it's complete, no matter how long or how short, it's done. Just the way I look at it. We have to do the best we can while we're here. It's all that we can do."

Skippy had hopped down off the truck and came to my side. I gave him a little pat and saw Coach smile.

"Let's get you back home," he said. "You got your Momma a good meal for tonight. Treat her right. She's been worried about you. Remember, she's hurting too. Can't hold anything said against each other during this time."

Getting in the passenger side, I glanced over at him. Immediately, I understood Momma had been talking with him.

Turning the ignition, he added one more thing.

"I expect to see you tomorrow. The boys are planning on shooting hoops after school, and I want you there. Trust me. It will make you feel better. You need to be around people that care…and you don't want me to find you over at Ricky's again."

* * * *

Starting back to school wasn't easy, but I made it through the first day. It was harder still to go to the gym after the last bell, but I got the overwhelming feeling like I had come home the minute I stepped onto the court.

1965-1966 Season

Chapter Nine

I found an escape in books. My English teacher assigned us the Tale of Two Cities. Afterward, I began reading any book I could get my hands on in the library. I even started going into the town library in Booneville. I wouldn't tell anyone where I was going, but Grandma caught on pretty quickly.

Soon enough, I was bringing back books for her to read. She favored those Reader's Digest condensed books, and I discovered James Bond wasn't only in the movies. I lost myself in the spy series. Though, I will admit I loved the movies based the books. I found myself debating with Grandma about who was the better movie actor—Sean Connery or John Wayne.

She loved John Wayne. We went out to the drive-in when El Dorado was playing. The guys on the team had asked me to go. Instead of going with them, I watched it with Grandma and Momma. Didn't care if anybody ribbed me about it.

Grandma was one of those people that amazed me. She never seemed to let anything get her down. She never complained, nor did she question why bad things happened to her. I mean, Grandpa had died years ago and now Troy, not to mention that her health was bad. Yet, she didn't even let losing a leg stop her.

Once, I asked her how she could be so strong. She said simply *faith*. I wished I had that kinda faith. I hadn't even gone back to church since we buried my brother.

My grandma said I would find my strength again. My mother thought I was going to hell.

Coach Carver told me to be there for Momma. I tried, but there was something about us that always led to fights. Most times, we kinda just avoided each other.

Before going into high school, I didn't really hang out with anyone. That changed. Playing basketball, we guys were together all the time. Despite my efforts to push the world away, I couldn't do it playing for Coach.

At first, I only hung around the guys at school and gym. Then, I would go home to my room and books, but I found it increasingly hard to be alone.

The team picked up a new guy from Hills Chapel. Hills Chapel was a hop and a skip from New Site and only had a grammar school. Usually, the kids from Hills Chapel went to Booneville for high school, but Mickey Strange had decided to come to New Site.

Mickey fit in with us well enough, I supposed. Larry seemed to think so. Didn't take long for the two of them to become inseparable. It didn't bother me much because I always turned Larry down when he wanted me to sneak into the pool hall out in Booneville or drive around the park out there.

When Troy had told me he was going into the military, he said he knew I wouldn't be alone because I would have my teammates. It was the reason he didn't worry about me when he was gone. He knew I would be fine.

Funny thing was Larry and Mickey wouldn't stop pestering me about hanging out with the team. At times I wanted to, but I just couldn't, not yet.

Starting high school, I began to notice that Coach not only helped his players out but his students as well. In homeroom, Mrs. Martin sent me down to the office with her morning attendance sheet when I saw Coach talking to Loretta Sneed's sister, Betty, outside her classroom. Passing by them, I heard Coach clearly as he handed her a can of tough skin that we used to wrap ankles.

"Spray it on a Q-tip and apply it to the cold sore. It will dry it right up."

I'll admit I thought it was a little odd until Betty won the annual beauty pageant. Loretta told me in English class that Betty gave credit to Coach Carver.

"Betty thought she would have to withdraw. She had the biggest cold sore. In Coach's American history class, Betty flunked a pop test...which wasn't like her at all. Coach stopped her after class and asked what was wrong. Betty broke down in tears and pointed to the cold sore. She told him about Momma spending a fortune on her dress and the pageant was only three days away. Well, by golly, it cleared right up, and she won," Loretta stated with pride in her sister.

At first, school had been a diversion from my grief. I found, though, there were days that I couldn't dismiss it. I began to struggle getting up in the morning and even walking into school. An overwhelming sadness had taken hold of me.

I was off my game. Coach had said that grieving would come in waves. I reckoned this was one of those days when it felt like a tidal wave. I was trying to act like everything was normal, but it wasn't.

Sitting in algebra class, I heard a knock on the door. Mr. Rushing opened it to find Coach requesting if he could see me for a moment. Pulling a student out of class wasn't unusual for Coach. Troy had told me last year he'd spent more time talking to Coach about his play and other ball teams than he had in class.

"Come on out to the gym," Coach said. "Gonna work on your shot."

I thought I was in for a lecture. I didn't really want to talk to anyone, but I didn't protest. I followed him.

The gym was empty. He picked up a ball and bounced it a couple of times. Throwing it to me, he said, "All you have to do today is breathe."

The rest of the time he spent on correcting my shot. Coach had a specific way he wanted you to shoot. Elbow toward the goal, with enough arch, pop the wrist straight down and keep your eyes on the basket.

There were about ten minutes before the bell when he left me in the gym by myself. The gym seemed empty and eerily quiet. Shooting around the horn, I made a basket from the far-right corner. Suddenly, the memory of Troy playing overwhelmed me. I cried.

My tears dried, but strangely, I felt better. Afterward, if I was having a bad day, I would ask Coach if I could have a few minutes alone in the gym. He would work a time out for me.

Once again, basketball became my release. When I had a ball in my hand, I felt I had a measure of control. More surprising was I found a release of my grief with running.

Troy had warned me it was hard getting in shape for the season. He didn't really have to tell me, because I saw it when I watched practices. Coach ran his players. I mean, he ran them hard.

I found there was pain in running to your limit. It's what I wanted —going to the brink of feeling like your lungs would burst, and then, breaking through that wall, and continuing to run.

When I ran, I could hear Troy. *The reason we won is that we were in better shape than any other team we played.* There was power in knowing that at the end of a game, when other teams were sucking wind, we wouldn't be.

Being on Coach's team, I discovered I wasn't the only one that lived, breathed, and ate basketball. Basketball was all-consuming for each of us.

Our team had changed from last year's championship team. We had graduated a lot of good ballplayers, including Donnie and Troy. Coach said we were going to be young this year.

We had only two seniors: Earl Bailey and Skeeter Williams, a new guy that had moved in from Belmont over the summer. Jimmy and Barry were returning juniors along with Paul Sharpe.

Our goal was another championship.

"Gonna be a challenge to be where we were last year," Coach said. "But nothing good comes easy. We're going back."

I'll admit I had my doubts, but none I would express. Coach seemed pretty confident, and no one I knew would question him.

I reckoned most times we might have been thrilled to have Skeeter become a Royal. He was tall at six-four, but Larry said not to get too excited.

"Jimmy said he heard Skeeter only made the B-team for Belmont," Larry said in my confidence. "Said the Belmont coach told him he wasn't good enough to play for them."

Afterward, Larry didn't have to be worried I'd tell anyone. I heard the same thing about twenty times when Skeeter made his first appearance at school. Everyone was talking about him.

At practice, you couldn't mistake him. The tall, lanky boy walked up to Coach. "I want to play ball."

Coach nodded his head. "It won't be easy." He gestured over to us guys. "Ask them. It's hard."

"I don't mind none," Skeeter said. "Just want to play."

I wondered if Skeeter knew what he was getting himself into...I mean, he was a senior. How did he expect to play for us if he didn't even make Belmont's team?

Skeeter was awkward at first and had a hard time getting the plays down. But like he had said, he just wanted to play. He worked hard, and soon enough, he was part of our team.

Not long after my shooting session with Coach, I stayed late to play one-on-one with Larry and Mickey. Larry was developing into a steady point guard, but I could take him one-on-one. Mickey and I went back and forth on who would win. Mickey could shoot the eyes off the ball, but I took pride in my defense as I always had.

After our last game, I wiped the sweat from my forehead. Taking a deep breath, I swallowed hard. "I heard that The Sons of Katie Elder is playing at Booneville. Was wondering if you guys were going."

Larry nodded. "Matter of fact, I was just going to ask you to come with us. The guys are going Saturday, even Jimmy. He just broke up with Donna. Said he was tired of being told he couldn't hang out with us. So, it will be the entire team. You can go with Mickey and me."

"You're driving?" I asked Larry. Not because I questioned, he could drive. I had been driving since I was ten, like most everyone else around here. It was only that Momma only let me drive to the store, never out town. We wouldn't get our driving license until next year.

"Don't be silly," Mickey answered for him. "I am."

* * * *

Life settled into a new norm. There was a gloom that still hung in the air at home, but it was lifting to reveal a grim acceptance of life without Troy.

Momma had started taking Grandma back to the beauty shop every Thursday, and nothing came between Momma and church. She was there every Sunday morning and evening, along with Wednesday service.

I hadn't gone back. I supposed at some point I would. It just wasn't yet.

Momma and I didn't talk much, but she would ask me about school and ball when she got home from work. For us, that was pretty good.

One Wednesday evening, I had just finished the dishes when I caught sight of headlights making their way up the drive. I knew it was Momma and Grandma getting back from church.

Putting the dish towel down, I went out to help Grandma out of the car. Momma could do it on her own, but it was easier if I helped get Grandma into the house.

The moment I walked out the screen door, I heard them arguing.

"Ain't right," Grandma said.

Momma stepped out of the car and sighed heavily like she had been dealing with Grandma for a spell. "Now, Mother, I'm sure it's not like that."

"Like what?" I asked, opening up the back door to get Grandma's crutch. She used it when she went to church. Her wheelchair was cumbersome and hard to transport especially because we didn't have a truck.

Grandma grimaced. "Your Momma doesn't believe me, but I heard it from Mildred McGillicutty. I swear it is quite disturbing."

"What?" I asked again. "What has got you so upset?"

"Well, if you must know," Grandma pressed her lips tightly together and shook her head. "I didn't know that Coach Carver is sending his children to school at *Booneville*."

I gave Momma a puzzled look. She shrugged. "Don't ask. It's got nothing to do with nothing."

"Nothing?" Grandma's voice rose. "He should have his kids at New Site."

"Mother, it's his decision. I'm sure he has his reasons. Now, don't get yourself all worked up. Coach's heart is all Royals."

"I don't know," Grandma whispered under her breath. "You know that Booneville let in those *Negroes* this year."

Momma threw her hands up in the air like there was no reasoning with Grandma and walked into the house. Grandma didn't stop rattling on about Coach's daughters going to school with blacks.

I didn't see a problem. Though I didn't really have anything to compare it to, being as there were no Negroes living in New Site. I had heard integration had begun in Mississippi, but around here, it didn't seem to be that big of a deal. I was surprised to hear Grandma talk like that.

Though, sometimes I think Grandma thought the Civil War was still going on. I did know she had strong feelings against Yankees and carpetbaggers.

Helping Grandma back into the house, she kept on ranting about how the world was going to hell. I left her to watch TV.

I walked down the hall to my room. I had a new Louis L'Amour book to read, but for some reason, I stopped outside of Troy's door. I didn't believe anyone had been inside since he died, or at least, I hadn't.

Turning the door handle, I went in and flicked on the light. For a brief moment, I thought Troy would walk in and yell at me for being in his room. It was as he left it that fateful night. His ball bag was in the corner. His letter jacket hung on a hanger on the closet door. His basketball awards were on the wall.

But there was no Troy. There was only silence.

Someone had thrown a see-through plastic bag on the bed. I looked at it for a long moment. It looked like what he wore the night he died.

Picking the bag up, I recognized the shirt he had worn covered in blood. His blood. *Why wouldn't Momma have thrown it out?*

My curiosity got the best of me. I opened it up and took out the clothes and shoes. Then, something dropped on the floor. I leaned over, picked up a small jewelry box, and opened it—a ring, a solitaire diamond. *Oh, Good Lord, it was an engagement ring.* A sudden flash of Troy getting ready for his date swept through me. He had been so excited.

"I didn't know what to do with it."

Looking over at the door, I saw Momma. "Troy was going to ask Missy to marry him?"

"He didn't, though," she said. "It was in his pocket."

"Troy didn't have time, Momma," I said. "With everything that happened when he got over to her house, he just didn't have time. Does Missy know?"

Momma shook her head. "I couldn't tell her." Her voice shook. "She got him killed…"

Her voice carried the anger I knew so well. Like Momma, I held my own anger toward Missy. If not for her, Troy wouldn't have been trying to lift a car off Missy's sister. Troy would be alive.

Yet, something didn't sit well with me about keeping the ring from her.

I walked over and put the ring in the top drawer of his dresser. "I think we should burn his clothes, Momma. Does no good keeping them around."

For once, she agreed with me. "I'll take care of it tomorrow."

Happy I didn't have to do it. I walked out of the room and left Momma with her thoughts.

* * * *

The Friday before the season was to start, I decided to try a cup of coffee. It seemed like everyone I knew drank it. I had never been allowed to before, but Grandma told me I could drink it if it were black. I tried it and spat the coffee out—nasty stuff.

Instead, I made a glass of iced tea and grabbed a PopTart. There was a beep. I was going to be late for school if I didn't get a move on it.

The opening game for our new season was next Tuesday. I found I was excited for basketball to start in earnest.

Being a freshman, I didn't expect I would be playing a lot for the A-team, but I should get plenty of playing time on the B-team. The expectation of winning another State championship was strong. I wanted nothing more than to win at least one while I was in high school.

In his car, Jimmy was ready to beep again when I ran out of the screen door. I hadn't even closed the door when he was backing up. When we got there, the bell had already rung for homeroom.

Parking, we both winced. There would be no sneaking inside. In his New Site jacket, Coach Carver was at his truck with the tailgate down. He gestured for us to come over.

Thought for sure we were in trouble. Instead, he gave us each a box.

"Got the new uniforms in today."

We followed him into the gym and set the boxes down in the locker room. Coach Carver took one out, a brilliant white, trimmed in red, with the number fourteen. He threw it to me.

I choked up. It had been Troy's number.

"What about me, Coach?" Jimmy asked.

"You'll get yours with everybody else after practice. You can leave yours here until then, too, Dean," Coach said. "Now, you two, get on out of here."

Jimmy took off. I started but turned back around. "Coach?"

Coach stopped checking out the uniforms and looked at me. "Something wrong?"

"Not for sure," I scratched my head. "Thought maybe I could talk to you about it…if that's okay. It's not about basketball."

"I've got time, son. What's up?"

Instantly, I regretted saying anything. I felt kinda foolish, but I knew Coach wouldn't let go of it once I had said something.

Hemming and hawing for a second, I began, "It's just something that Grandma said the other night…about you sending your kids to Booneville for school instead of New Site." I paused for a long moment. "She said they have blacks."

Coach frowned. With the look he gave me, I wanted to sink into the floor.

"Do blacks bother you?"

Shaking my head, I responded honestly. "No, sir, but I don't know any. It's just it upset Grandma mightily."

He nodded as if he understood. "I'll tell you, Dean, I have my reasons for sending my girls out to Booneville. The decision had absolutely nothing to do with anything other than I wanted my kids to work for what they get.

"But I think what you're telling me is that your grandma is more upset that I chose a school that is integrated. For that, I make no apology. I have learned it is best in life to judge a man by his actions and not by the color of his skin." Coach drew in a deep breath and went on. "Do you have a problem with that?"

"No, sir." I wished I had never mentioned it. "Can I go now?"

"As soon as you tell me what is really bothering you."

Stunned, I had been ready to leave and lament my lack of judgment. Now, I stood speechless with my mouth hanging open. The man had an uncanny ability to read my mind.

"Sit down," Coach said. "You're not leaving until you tell me."

I did as I was told. Pressing my lips tightly together, I thought long and hard how to find the words. I didn't want Coach to think any worse of me than he already did, but I needed his advice.

Looking down at the floor, I said, "I think that Troy was going to ask Missy to marry him the night he died. I found a ring."

He rubbed his chin. "Missy doesn't know, I take it."

"I don't think so." I shook my head. "Momma couldn't bring herself to give it to Missy...and I...I think she's right. Troy would be alive if not for Missy."

The words spoken gave Coach a glimpse of the darkness in my heart—darkness, I had yet to see the light to find my way out. I didn't dare look up and see the disappointment in his eyes.

"You blame Missy for his death." Coach said the words as a statement, not a question. "You don't need me to tell you that's unfair to her. You're hurting at the loss of your brother, but Troy's death was an accident."

I sprang up and waved my hands in front of my face. My anger unleashed. "But Missy sent him after her sister. She made him...and he died."

Slowly, Coach shook his head. "Troy made the decision to help. He did—because he was a good, good man. He was helping someone in need. He would have done it for anyone he saw in a car accident because that was who he was."

Grimacing, I sat in silence and stewed in my thoughts. *Troy's death wasn't an accident. Missy caused it.*

Coach slid the box of uniforms over and sat on the bench.

"Anger festers, Dean, and does no one any good. Right now, you find it easier to direct that anger at Missy than to deal with the fact that maybe, just maybe, it wasn't

110

anyone's fault. There was no one to blame, just a horrid accident. But if you want advice, I think it's pretty simple."

I lifted my head and looked straight at him. "Yeah, what would that be?"

"What would Troy have wanted you to do?"

For a long moment, I sat without saying a word. Coach got up and patted me on the back.

"You're a good kid, Dean. It hasn't been easy for you lately, but I promise, doing the right thing will make you feel better."

* * * *

Momma and I had a long talk. In the end, Momma invited Missy over to dinner after church on Sunday.

Grandma cooked fried chicken, gravy, biscuits—my favorite meal. But I can't say I was that hungry. I had lost my appetite.

When Missy knocked on the door, I admit I had second thoughts about this gathering to discuss Troy. Yet, my doubts evaporated the moment I saw her.

She was dressed up real nice in a belted green dress, and she had done up her hair. However, her reddened eyes betrayed she had been crying.

Immediately, she said, "I'm sorry...so, so sorry."

There were a lot of tears.

It didn't take long to learn that Troy's death devasted Missy. She blamed herself more than Momma and I ever could. Her life had been in an upheaval. Her sister, Stephanie, had survived, but was severely injured and was still recovering. Stephanie's deadbeat husband had left her. Her parents had taken Stephanie back into the house. Her mother had to quit work to care for her.

Missy gave up her desire to become a nurse and had dropped out of Northeast. She now worked as a cashier at Walden's Grocery in Booneville.

She was miserable.

When Momma showed Missy the ring, Missy broke down. Momma and Missy hugged for a long time.

Missy placed the ring on the table. "Thank you for showing me."

"It's yours, Missy," I picked it up and gave it back to her. "Troy wanted you to have it. I know he did. When he left that evening, he was so excited. Looking back, I should have guessed what he had in mind."

"He told me you were the one for him," Momma said, smiling at Missy.

I didn't know if that was true or not, but Momma had changed her tune about Missy. Guess I had too.

The rest of the visit was spent sharing tales about Troy. Grandma told stories that I hadn't even heard about antics Troy did when he was a baby. As much as we cried, we laughed. It felt good to talk about my brother and remember him with someone who loved him as we loved him.

Afterward, there was a bond that developed between Momma and Missy. I supposed it was the grief they shared.

When my season started the next Tuesday, Momma and Missy were in the stands together.

Chapter Ten

Driving toward the basket, I laid in the lay-up.

Coach Carver blew his whistle. "Dean, what did I say? To the left. You hafta go left. Do it again."

I swiped my forehead. Sweat poured from me. It was only the fifth time Coach had me running the exact same play. It wasn't exactly easy for me to drive left. My instinct was to go right.

Larry took the ball at the top of the key. He dribbled once and threw it to me. This time, I put the ball down to the left side. Immediately, Jimmy stole it.

Once again, Coach blew his whistle. Frowning, he walked over to me. "Throw the ball back to Larry," he told Jimmy. "Now, Dean, watch." Larry threw Coach the ball. Coach faked right, went left for a dribble, then went up for a jump shot. "That's what I want."

I nodded, trying to hide my frustration.

We had a big game coming up on Friday night against East Union. Coach had gone over the scouting report with us. Seemed like this kid, Franklin, was their big shooter. A forward, the kid was a lefty and set up on the left side. He always, always went left for a jump shot.

Today, I was supposed to be this Franklin at practice. It's what I did mostly as a freshman, to get the A-team ready for games. I didn't get much playing time for the games. Coach said that what we were doing was important.

Each player had their role. At the moment, this was mine.

I guess I wouldn't have been so frustrated if I had gotten more playing time. I only got to play for half the game on the B-team.

The team had picked up where we left off last year. We had only lost one game, and that was to Corinth, by one point.

"Discipline and focus," Coach drove into us. "This is our game. We play it our way."

Stepping back into position, I listened to Coach instruct Larry to go again. The ball came to me, and I went left.

* * * *

Sitting at the end of the bench, Virgil handed me a towel. The B game had just gotten over. J.C., Mickey, Virgil, and I would turn around and play for the A-team.

I didn't need the towel. Don't think Virgil did neither. I mean Coach only let us play two quarters. We didn't break a sweat.

There was a certain irritation in me. We had lost. The way I figured it, we wouldn't have if J.C., Mickey, Virgil, and I had played the whole game. East Union had a firecracker shooter. Lit the eyes off the basket, but Virgil, J.C., and Mickey didn't complain. I wasn't about to act like it bothered me, even though it did.

I felt like Coach didn't care about the B team. I couldn't stand to lose, especially when we should have won.

With the A game about to start, the starting five for both teams lined up for the jump ball as the tallest player for each readied to leap for possession. Coach Carver gestured to one of the officials before the guy had a chance to toss the ball. Mickey nudged me as Coach reached for his rulebook in his back pocket.

"This is going to be good," Mickey said.

Watching East Union's coach come off the bench, I heard him muttering. "Lord have mercy on us. What now?"

The two officials, along with the two coaches, huddled together for a few minutes. Coach Carver took a step back and nodded to himself as one of the officials pointed to one of East Union's boys to sit down.

Confused, the kid lowered his head and shrugged as he took a seat on the bench. The East Union coach pointed to another player who checked into the game.

Sitting to my left, Mickey leaned over. "That's the kid who just played against us."

Mickey was right. The kid was the one who had the hot hand, but it didn't explain why he was taken out before the whistle even blew. I mean, lots of guys played in the B game and went on to play in the main competition.

The game went off without another hitch. Sure enough, the player Jimmy had on defense went left every time he got the ball. Jimmy was right there on the kid. The guy got flustered, and even when he was open, he couldn't hit a shot.

We were winning the game just like Coach had game planned.

Playing for Coach Carver, I had discovered a huge difference between being in the stands watching the game and being a part of his team. As a fan, you had to judge the man by the results his team had on the court. As a player, I had only just begun to understand what it took to win.

Beyond the score, I also began to realize that fans interrupted the results differently. Around New Site, whatever Coach Carver said was gospel. Outside our community, fans didn't feel the same way. As a matter of fact, they had pretty strong feelings about him.

When the final buzzer rang, I heard whisperings amid the East Union fans. As they walked by us, I heard them mutter under their breath. *Cheater. Ruthless. Win at all costs. Not worth it selling your soul to the devil.*

Our family and fans were ecstatic. *Brilliant. Smartest coach around. Prepared. Understands what it takes to win a game. Have faith in Coach.*

Getting dressed in the locker room, I still didn't understand exactly what Coach did that made the other team so mad, but the way I saw it, Coach just knew the rules better. He had pulled out his worn-out rulebook and went right to the spot to show the ref whatever he was claiming.

Personally, I thought it was kinda funny that Coach knew the rules better than anyone. Besides, the other fans couldn't have known how hard we worked to win.

As I was untying my shoes, Larry plopped down beside me.

"You know what it was?"

"No. Tell me."

Larry grinned real broad. "Jimmy said he overheard Coach talking to Mr. Jones after the game. You can't play more than four quarters in a night, whether in the B or A game. The guy played all four quarters in the B game. Can't do that."

I smiled. Then a thought struck me. *That's why Coach doesn't play us more than two quarters. He may need us.*

Zipping up my gym bag, I realized that I had a lot to learn, but the most important lesson to grasp— I needed to trust Coach. He had a reason for every move he made.

For some silly reason, the realization made me feel important. I was part of the New Site Royals. I walked out of the locker room with a skip in my step.

* * * *

Walking into the gym this evening, I felt pretty good. The season had gone well. We had only lost four games. One loss was against the team we were about to face. A couple of weeks ago, Jumpertown Cardinals had beat us with a scrawny little guard who wrangled down thirty-five points.

We were set to avenge that loss on our home court. Coach hadn't been happy letting one kid single-handedly beat us.

The player hadn't been on Coach's scouting reports the first time we'd faced them. Coach said later that the guy was a sophomore and hadn't started until the night we played the Cardinals, but tonight number fifteen for Jumpertown was in our sights.

At practice, I pretended to be him. I learned his moves. Coach said our opponent had soft hands and a nice touch, but the game would be ours if we shut him down.

From tip-off, the Cardinal guard with a military-style crew cut was continually frustrated. Jimmy was in his face on every shot, guarding him tight. If they tried to set up a pick, then Barry would pick him up on the slide. By the third quarter, the game was ours.

Most of Jumpertown thought so as well. They began to slack off, stopped blocking out on rebounds, and stopped hustling after loose balls, except for that guard. This guy wouldn't stop scrapping for the ball.

Coach sent J.C. and me out at the beginning of the fourth quarter. We were leading by twenty-one. J.C. was supposed to take the guy, but something about him annoyed me.

"Can I take him, Coach?"

"You want him, you've got him." Coach Carver said.

I stuck to him like glue. He was like an annoying little ant that wouldn't stop going for food. Jumpertown shot and I blocked him out on the boards. The ball bounced away from us, and we both dove for the loose ball and head-butted each other.

The ref called a time out. It took a moment for us to get to our feet. To my surprise, the guy walked over to me and patted my back.

"You okay?"

I nodded. He gave me a small smile and walked back to his team. For a brief moment, I considered going to the bench when Coach Carver asked me if I was okay. Then, I saw the back of that guard. He was ready to go.

"I'm fine," I replied. "I want to play."

The game may not have been in doubt, but the two of us began playing our own one-on-one game. I scored a few high-percentage shots, and once I did an up-fake and drove for two.

I can't say my opponent had the night I did, but there again, he didn't have the teammates I had. Even us on the second team had a connection.

The coach instructed us to shut him down. We did.

The guy only scored three points, and his team lost by nineteen.

Yet, I was still irritated with him. We dominated the game, but he played every second he was out there like the game was still on the line. *Didn't he realize he was beaten?*

Afterward, Coach was pleased with the win, but he focused us on our next game in his usual manner. I dressed and walked out of the locker room behind Mickey and Larry.

I didn't get three feet out of the locker room when the Cardinal guard came walking up to me. He had his Jumpertown jacket on and his gym bag in his hand.

"Hey, man." He extended his hand to me. "Rich Harden. Just wanted to make sure you weren't hurt when we banged heads."

"Nay, I'm fine, and you?"

"My head's okay." Rich patted his chest. "My heart is another matter. Hard loss."

"You beat us the first time. Matter of fact, you torched us up. You had to have known coming to New Site…"

"I know…I know," he smiled broadly. "Lucky to have beat you guys the first time. Coach Carver doesn't let you beat him a second time."

I had to chuckle on that remark. "Guess you can say that."

"Give my right arm to be coached by him. You guys are going to do it again this year. I feel it. You're going to win State."

I almost said that was our goal, but I caught myself. I just nodded.

"You guys are winners. Gotta go catch the bus. Good luck," Rich turned and walked away, but I swore I heard him add under his breath. "I'm gonna be a winner, too."

Larry walked over to me. "What did he want?"

"Nothing much." I shrugged. "Asked about my head. Told him I had a hard one. So, it wasn't a problem."

"Then what's the matter?"

I hadn't noticed that I was still staring at the Cardinal guard. I shook my head. "Nothing."

"Let's go." Larry nudged me.

Smiling, I turned back to my buddies. Mom and Missy were waiting for me. Catching sight of them, I could tell they were happy for me.

Guess I had a pretty good night.

* * * *

The lights dimmed; the game had been played.

It seemed strange to me that a year had passed since Troy had won the State championship. Here I was standing in the center of the coliseum in Jackson. This was what it was like playing in the tournament of champions.

Once more, the Royals had taken the Class B State crown with a win over Houlka at Brookhaven. Once more, we had fallen in the semi-finals of the Grand Slam, again against Pelahatchie. This time an outbreak of the flu did us in, but Coach said not to make excuses. As a team, we refused to fold and fought hard throughout the game.

Coach was proud of us. I'm sure he was especially of Skeeter. The guy that couldn't make Belmont's team had worked really hard. So much so, Skeeter made All-State.

To some, my role in this championship may have seemed small. I was a bench player who came in when the game was in hand.

Yet, I felt I was more.

I had done everything Coach asked of me. I had helped prepare the starting five for the games. Mostly, the guys felt like family to me. We pushed each other and picked each other up when the ball didn't bounce our way.

The year had been hard, but the guys helped me through it.

We had come close to winning it all, but I was hungry. I wanted more. Before the game, Coach said it was important to have a dream and never lose sight of that dream.

To win two championships in a row had been hard. Some said improbable. But here we stood.

During the year, Coach had drilled into us. "You have to believe in yourself as much as you do in your teammates."

With each game, I had felt that belief. Yet, there was more. That belief expanded into our community. They were proud of us.

Standing here, I felt what could have been…what we could have brought home to everyone.

A sudden thought struck me. We had come here satisfied winning our State title, but could we do the impossible?

An impossible dream stirred within me. I had a sudden realization—that the overall title could be ours. I didn't only want to get to the Grand Slam; I wanted to win it.

1966-67 Season

Chapter Eleven

Sweat poured off me. The guys and I had been playing two-on-two for an hour. We came to the gym most nights after working for the day.

School had let out less than a week ago. Jimmy, Larry, and I had been helping Coach out in his pepper patch the last few days, but I was going to work for Old Man Sanders on his farm for the rest of the summer. Mickey was helping his dad out on their farm.

No matter what we were doing during the day, we congregated at the gym after supper... all of us. I imagined that Troy would have been happy that I had what he wanted for me.

I realized that Coach watched over me. If I had a problem, he was there. The guys and I were close. I wasn't on the outside, but part of this team.

Neither Grandma nor Momma asked where I was going. They knew and didn't have to worry about me.

Pivoting around Larry, I drove hard toward the basket. Mickey planted himself in front of me. I crashed into him, and he toppled back. My shot rolled in, but Mickey laughed.

"Charge," he said. "Basket doesn't count."

Extending my hand to help him back up, I was fixing to argue the point, but my eyes caught sight of a guy walking into the gym. I studied him for a minute.

Dressed in shorts and a T-shirt, he wore sneakers like he was ready to play. He was shorter than I was, probably around five-nine or ten. His dark hair was cut in a crew-cut; he had an athletic built.

I recognized him.

He was that Cardinal guard.

"Hey, guys," he said. "Coach Carver said that I would find you guys down here."

Looking over at Larry, I realized that he was as confused as I was. Then Jimmy stepped forward. "Yeah, Coach said that you might be coming down, but didn't expect you tonight. Didn't you just move today?"

"Didn't want to waste any time."

Jimmy turned to the rest of us. "We got a new player this year. Rich Harden's family has moved to New Site."

* * * *

Waking up this morning, I found it hard to get up. Outside, the day promised to be a nice one. The sun was shining, and the birds were singing, but it did nothing to alleviate my bad mood.

Besides, Larry was late. I wanted to leave before Momma got up to get ready for church. She wanted me to go today.

"Are you going to be gone all day?" Grandma asked.

"Na," I replied, turning back to her. She was in her usual spot on the porch. She loved that old rocking chair. "Just this morning, I suppose. Some of the guys are taking me fishing with Coach."

She nodded. It wasn't a good day for her neither. A year earlier, Troy had died.

I hadn't thought the day would affect me like it was. I mean, the grief hadn't gone away. Coach had been right when he told me that there would be times when a wave of pain would come out of nowhere and overwhelm you. This morning, a sadness gripped me that wouldn't let go.

"You know you should be going to church," Grandma said when Larry pulled into the driveway. "Make you feel better."

Shrugging, I didn't disagree with her. Maybe it would have. Instead, I went over and kissed her cheek. "Say a prayer for me."

She patted my hand. "I always do."

With a deep sigh, I hopped off the porch and into Larry's car. He had two fishing poles in the back seat. Good thing, because I didn't have one that worked. The lines were all tangled up. It had been a long while since I had fished.

"You got any worms?" I asked.

"Yeah, Dad got some yesterday at Massey's Store. They're fine. He put them in the frig. Momma would have had his head if she had known, but he hid 'em behind the milk." Larry nodded. "Told ya didn't have to worry about a thing this morning except yourself."

I smiled. Larry had always been a good friend.

"Picking up Mickey?"

"Yep, but first I said I would pick up Rich."

Larry glanced over at me. I don't suppose I hid my disappointment well.

"Stop frowning. Rich is a good guy," Larry said. "Don't know why you don't like him."

I felt my frown deepen. Couldn't put my finger on the exact reason, except Rich annoyed me. He had been here no more than a week. He was always going on about how lucky we were and what a great coach we had.

Couldn't dispute that Rich was a good ballplayer. Quick and agile, he played with his heart. The guy was stubborn and determined. Didn't care who he faced, he thought he was going to win.

I reckoned it rubbed me the wrong way that all he had to do was tell dear old Dad he wanted to play for Coach

Carver and his dad moved to New Site. Just didn't seem right to me.

A lot of players would have loved to play for Coach—he was well-respected in the community, and state for that matter—but that didn't mean they just upped and moved to New Site. Just not the way it was done.

Driving down the road, Larry made a turn toward Mr. Jones' farm. Our principal had a large farm not far from the school. I knew Mr. Jones grew cotton and soybeans, but he also had a large herd of Angus cattle.

We drove past it and came to one of Mr. Jones's sharecropper's houses. The timeworn wooden house was about half a mile down from the farm. The lawn had been freshly mowed, and there was an old truck parked in front of the open front porch. Reminded me of the home I grew up in, except it didn't have an outhouse.

From the look of it, it had only two bedrooms, which seemed surprising since there were three small children playing in the front, and I saw that a couple of older kids were feeding chickens in the back.

The screen door opened, and a woman stepped outside. I supposed she was around my Momma's age. Thin, with her hair pulled tightly off her face, she smiled. Another child rounded her legs, a toddler.

"Hi, ma'am," Larry said, getting out of the car. "Looking for Rich. Is he around?"

Covering her eyes from the sun, she pointed up toward the farm. "He's helping his dad out, but it looks like he's seen you."

Larry and I looked over and saw Rich running through the pasture and ducking under the fence. Larry turned back to Mrs. Harden.

"Nice to meet you, ma'am. I'm Larry, and this is Dean."

I had made my way out of the car and nodded politely. She seemed quite pleasant, although tired, but having just moved with so many kids would explain it.

How many siblings did Rich have? Why didn't anyone tell me? Here I had thought that Rich was some spoiled brat. A know-it-all. I had been wrong.

"I've heard so much about you," Mrs. Harden said. "Rich has been so excited about this move. He talks about you guys all the time."

"We're excited he moved here," Larry said.

Rich ran up to us. "Let me grab my lunch." He made a small wave. "I'll be right back."

Larry and I got back in the car.

"How many kids are there?" I asked as I closed the door.

"Counting Rich, I heard there's twelve, but he has three siblings that have already graduated and are on their own."

Our conversation ended with Rich hopping in the back seat.

"Let's go." Rich placed his paper sack beside him. "It looks like a good day to fish."

* * * *

Coach Carver was already at his dad's farm when we pulled up. Coach had his hands full with a tackle box and a couple of rod and reels. His young towhead son, Joey, followed close behind his father as Skippy ran along the path down to the lake.

I reckoned Joey was around four of five. In the off season, Coach brought his son with him most places. Guess it helped his wife out with the kids. She had had another baby not long ago.

Watching them, I felt suddenly envious of the little kid. I had always wanted a father to do things with me like fishing. Instead, my only memories of my dad were filled with being smacked across the face for no reason other than

I was in the room. There had been once Dad had taken his belt to me so bad that Momma had thrown herself across me to get him to stop. It had stopped my beating, but not hers.

My good memories were of Troy, my older brother who looked after me. Despite being four years older, he would take me outside and play basketball until Dad passed out. Our basketball court hadn't been much, only a small patch of backyard dirt. The hoop had no net and was attached to an old white oak tree with a backboard made from worn planks. Yet, it had been my refuge.

Now, Troy was gone. He had been gone a year. The thought tore at me and the pain seemed unbearable.

"Dean, come on down here," Coach said. He placed his tackle box down. "This should be a good spot."

I nodded and had to smile. Joey stood with a couple of worms in his hands trying to give one to me. He just couldn't seem to find which end to pick up.

Casting my reel out, I stood and watched my bobber while the other guys arrived. There was something to be said about spending the morning fishing. The early morning air was fresh and brisk as a slight fog hung over the water. Weeping Willows fluttered in the breeze. It was a downright peaceful sight.

After half an hour, I couldn't say that any of us was having much luck. Nobody had caught anything. Coach laid his pole down.

"I'll be back in a minute," he said, heading back to the shed. "Come on Joey."

Reckoned Coach wasn't that patient of a fisherman. Then again, we weren't exactly being quiet. Don't think there was a true fisherman in the group of us. I swear Mickey couldn't stop talking if his life depended on it. Not to mention, Virgil brought his dog along who was swimming about a foot from us.

"Virgil, get that mongrel out of here." Jimmy pointed at the brown-haired mutt splashing around in the water. "He's done scared off any big 'uns."

"Don't think there's any fish here. I betcha the terrapins have eaten them all." Virgil said.

"Fish are here." From the corner of my eye, I saw it was Coach returning with a bucket in hand.

"Gotta have confidence. Otherwise, the fish can smell your doubt," Coach said.

J.C. laughed. "Think you got it wrong. It's horses that can sense your fear, Coach."

"Really?"

For a moment, J.C. thought Coach was serious. His face fell. We all burst into laughter. Took a minute, but J.C. caught on to the joke. Sure 'nough no fish were gonna bite today, with the racket we were making.

But Coach would never accept us going away empty-handed. Coach had done gone and gotten some fish food.

"Go ahead, Joey," Coach Carver said to his son as he placed the bucket down by his feet. "You can start throwing some in, but don't fall in the water."

As soon as the food was thrown, fish came biting. Rich caught the first one, about a foot and a half long. Perfect for eating.

We couldn't get our hooks baited fast enough. Waiting to get another worm, I watched Larry make a face while he baited his hook. Squinting, he opened his mouth wide and kinda went with the worm's movement wiggling and squirming around.

"What are you doing? Trying to dance with the bait?" I kidded with him.

"I just taught him how to lure the biggest fish," Larry chuckled. "You just watch."

Larry snapped back with rod and slung it forward, right into the weeping willow. "Doggone it."

Watching my bobber, I shook my head and chuckled.

Coach Carver moved over beside me. "You doing okay?"

I glanced around for a second and looked at everyone who had come to take my mind off what had happened a year ago. I nodded. "Yeah, I think I am."

"Good," he said. "You got a bite."

Jerking back my reel, I caught a big one. Turned out to be the biggest one of the day; around five pounds was Coach's guess. All and all, we caught twenty fish and threw back six.

"Do you want them?" Coach asked. "You get first pick."

Smiling, I shook my head. "What time is it?"

"Almost ten," Coach answered. "Do you need to go?"

I hesitated. I didn't want to appear ungrateful, but I had a sudden need to see Momma and Grandma. I mean, here I was feeling better than I had in a long time. I wanted them to feel the same.

"Momma wanted me to go to church…," I mumbled under my breath.

That look came across Coach's face, the one that seemed to know what you were thinking. "Then, I think you need to go."

J.C. lifted his hand toward me. "You can go with me. I promised my Momma I wouldn't miss."

It had been so long since I had gone to church, I had plumb forgot he went to the same church. We had even been baptized on the same day, at the revival when I was twelve. I had figured if J.C. had the courage to walk up there and say he wanted to get baptized, I could. I had been wanting to do it for a long time, fearing hell and damnation.

"Thanks."

We stopped off long enough to change our shirts and wash up a bit, but we were there right after the singing.

I knew Grandma would be in the last pew. It was easier for her to get in and out that way. I slipped in beside her and Mrs. Peeler. They had been friends since they were kids.

About three pews up, Momma turned around and saw me. She smiled and nodded, but not before I saw a tear roll down her cheek.

* * * *

Once again, the time had come for the new season to begin. I tied up my laces and was ready to play. I realized I wouldn't be starting, but in all likelihood, I'd be the first off the bench if anyone got into foul trouble.

Sitting beside me, Larry exhaled. "You ready?"

I only had time to nod. Coach walked into the locker room.

Coach looked at us with a subtle smile. "This is it, boys. Know before you go out on the court, that everyone we meet this year will be after us to prove a point—that we aren't as good as we think we are. We will be playing against everyone's best game.

"We have won State twice in a row, but that's in the past. Nothing we have done matters this year. This is a new season, but we know how to get there. We know what it takes to get it done—one game at a time.

"Tonight, our goal is to win—nothing else. Play your game. Let's get it done."

Taking the court, I smiled. There was nothing like the feeling of running out to our excited fans. Larry said that we had the best fans out there. He was right.

No matter where we went, our fans and community came with us. Our supporters paid for our meals when we went out after a game. Old man Sanders told Momma that he had sold a pig last year to make sure he contributed to the fund.

Breaking up into two lines for lay-ups, we took to the court, and the stands exploded with whoops and hollers. The Royals were back for another year.

Adrenaline flowed through my veins. I felt there was nothing I couldn't do.

Reckoned the guys felt the same. Our play exuded confidence. We started the season with a win. In his debut for New Site, Rich poured in twenty-nine points. Larry, who was now the starting guard, had ten. I got six, but Coach never dwelled on who scored the points.

Team was all that mattered. We followed Coach's game plan and won. If we lost, we lost as a team as well, but losing was the last thing on our minds.

Chapter Twelve

"Dang it." I threw my cards down. It was the third game in a row I lost.

Larry sat across from me and laughed. "You give your hand away with the look on your face."

Shaking my head, I sighed. "Well, I need to get home. Reckon Grandma will be wondering where I'm at."

"Like she don't know you're either at the gym or here at Massey's playing cards." Mickey scooped up the cards back into one stack and shuffled them. He placed them in the middle of the table.

It was only a board sitting on some cement blocks, but it worked out right nice to play cards. Jimmy's dad owned the place.

The white-washed general store sat to the east of the high school. Mr. Massey drove a school bus and let us come in after practice every afternoon and hang out.

"One more game," Mickey said. He didn't even wait for my answer before dealing the hand.

Shrugging, I picked up my cards. Mickey was always clowning around. Right near got him in hot water with Coach two nights ago during our game against Thrasher.

Mickey and I kinda exchanged being the first to go in when someone got into foul trouble. That night, it had been Mickey when Jimmy got his third foul in the second period. No sooner than Mickey got in, he got called for a foul going for a loose ball.

Going back down court after the free throws were shot, Mickey grinned and waved at Coach. Now, Coach wasn't the kind to pull anyone for making a mistake like missing a shot or throwing the ball away. Matter of fact, I couldn't remember a time that he had.

I had seen other coaches rip their players apart in front of all the spectators. Not Coach. I couldn't remember a time Coach humiliated a player. He would pull them aside where they could talk by themselves. I knew because he had done it to me when we played in the County Tournament.

It was in the game against Booneville. When I was throwing the ball in after they scored, I stepped on the line. Booneville got the ball back. I couldn't believe I had done something so stupid. I looked at Coach, who gestured with his hand to take it easy.

I played the rest of the game. Afterward, he talked to me. "Don't rush," he said. "You need to look where you are positioned on the court and think."

But that wasn't grinning and waving running down the court. Coach pulled Mickey and put me into the game. I didn't think Mickey would do that again. Coach didn't bother to say anything to Mickey after the game.

Larry said that Coach figured Mickey knew what he had done. I expected the same.

Looking at the cards in my hand, I noticed a man I didn't recognize enter the store. He walked in with Mr. Massey and talked loud enough for us to hear.

"I'm telling ya, Hershel. It's nothing but cheatin'."

Mr. Massey blew out a deep sigh as if he was exasperated. "Jack, ain't gonna argue with you. Coach Carver just outsmarts you guys. Stop being such an ass. Makes you look like a bad loser."

"I know you hide behind the *rules*, but something's not right about slowing the ball down like you guys do."

"It's called coaching. Our team is just more disciplined than you guys."

"Then whatcha gonna say when they find out Coach Carver recruited another player to play for you guys. Gonna get you guys suspended."

I don't remember getting up or how I got up to the front of the store, but I wasn't gonna let someone bad talk Coach.

"Mister, I don't know who you are, but we don't talk out of our butts around here," I began. "There is no one that knows the rules better than Coach…and if your problem is with Skeeter and Rich. I'll tell you for a fact…that Skeeter's family moved here…after he was cut from Belmont.

"Ain't Coach's fault Skeeter made the team and became an All-State player…and if you are talking of Rich…his father moved his family where he got a job," I said.

The man looked me up and down like I didn't amount to much. "You one of Carver's boys?"

"Yes, sir." I puffed out my chest and pulled my shoulders back. "I'm a Royal."

"I hear Coach Carver is pretty hard on you guys. Ain't he?"

Behind me, Larry and Mickey stood in silence, but I knew they were there in support. Nobody was going to talk like that about Coach around here. I shrugged it off with a laugh.

"We do what we have to, to win."

The man leaned toward us. "I hear he whips you good if you make a mistake. Treats you like you're in boot camp."

We didn't answer. We realized he was baiting us.

He gave us a little wink. "Come on, boys. Tell me, just between us. What's he like?"

Mickey took a step up. "Well, mister, if you must know, I'll put it like this: If Coach sends you for a 2x4, he doesn't want a damn 2x6."

Larry and I chuckled, but my good humor lasted only as long as a quick glance at the man. His face got red; his lips thinned.

"This isn't some kind of daggum joke…"

I could take no more. "Sounds like you're envious of our two State championships. I'll tell you what…if they had had the four divisions before '65 as they do now, we would have had two more State titles. We worked real hard for everything we've gotten. If you have a problem with that, then beat us, but I'll be honest, I don't think you can."

Mr. Massey smiled smugly. "Couldn't have said it better myself."

Gritting his teeth, the man grunted and left.

* * * *

Crouching down on my toes, I slid to my left and turned to head the player to his left. Coach had drilled into me that the guy only drove right.

We had played hard all season for this moment. For the third year, the Royals were in the state finals. This year, we were in a fight for our lives against Houlka.

The score had gone back and forth, but we were fighting more than our opponent. Every time we moved at a guy, we seemed to draw a foul.

Coach had hit his towel on the floor too many times to count. Yet, unlike his usual demeanor, he sat on his chair. He had been warned by the official not to get back up. Hadn't stopped him from directing us from the bench.

Earl fouled out early in the third quarter. Coach put me into the game. The first time down the court, Larry hit me on the right side. Defense didn't come out on me. I had a shot. Looking for a second, I hesitated and threw it back to Larry, who hit Jimmy in the middle. Double-teamed, he lost the ball.

After the next rebound, Coach called a time-out.

"Dean, they're giving you a clean shot. Take it."

We clapped and took back to the court. With my nervousness gone, I did just like Coach told me and got into position. Immediately, Larry passed the ball to me again. This time, I took one dribble to my right, shot a jump shot, and scored.

Running back down the court, Coach gave me a nod. Confidence gained. On our next possession, I did the same thing. By the third time, instead of the zone defense giving me an open shot, the guy came out on me, expecting me to shoot. Instead, I took a dribble and made a bounce pass inside to Jimmy. He scored.

I could feel the game shift. After that, their defense collapsed. With our offense in sync, Rich got a hot hand.

Houlka had no answer.

The buzzer sounded.

We held the trophy high in the air with our third straight State championship.

While celebrating, I saw Coach from the corner of my eye talking with the official that had given us trouble. I couldn't hear them, but I could see that it wasn't going well. Grimacing, Coach shook his head and walked off toward us.

His face broke into a broad smile as he moved into the celebratory crowd. Behind him, I watched the official frown. It was quite obvious he didn't care for Coach. With the way he called the game, he didn't like us much either.

Larry clasped my back. My attention turned back to our win, and the scene was forgotten. There was too much excitement. We had just won State.

The team drove in cars to Jackson and stayed at the Sun-'n-Sand Motel. I roomed with Mickey, Larry, and Virgil. Coach put one level-headed guy in each room. Larry was ours.

The previous year had been the first time I had stayed in a motel with the team. I'll admit I kinda liked it, but there again, I wasn't paying for it.

Having been there before, I knew just where the International House of Pancakes was: right next door. I loved breakfast almost as much as I loved basketball. I reckoned I couldn't rightly compare the two. Nothing came before ball, but those pancakes stacked with whipped cream on top and syrup pouring off the sides, well now, they tasted really good. We didn't have any of those places around home.

Each year, the state tournament was played at different places, but the Grand Slam was always played in Jackson. There was excitement going to Jackson that I can't put into words. My stomach would get all queasy but in a good way.

Coach said it was a feeling of accomplishment, which was all fine and good, but we came to play ball. This was our third trip down here. We had a lot to be proud of winning three State titles in a row. Yet, we hadn't made it to the finals of the Grand Slam.

This was where I had wanted to be last year…back here playing for it all.

We rested in our rooms until it was time to go. I was in Coach's car, along with the rest of my roommates. The other two cars were behind us.

After driving no more than ten minutes, we pulled into the coliseum's parking lot. I'll admit I felt kinda important. People were coming to see us play West Union this afternoon. That was the way it always was. Class B played Class BB, and Class A played Class AA.

We came to the entrance and stopped at the booth.

Coach Carver rolled down his window. "These three cars are New Site."

From the way Coach said it, it sounded like he didn't expect to pay. It was the way it was for the teams playing, not paying for parking or admission to the game. But I guess this attendant didn't see it that way.

"Fifty cents," the attendant said, then added. "For each car."

"No," Coach Carver said in a low deep voice. "You don't understand. We're one of the teams that are playing."

The attendant looked at Coach like he didn't believe him. He certainly didn't care who we were. He snickered. "Don't matter."

"You're telling me that the teams are paying to park?"

"The other teams drive in here on buses. Cars pay."

Larry and I exchanged looks. We both understood that Coach wasn't happy. His deepened voice was a clear indication of his temper brewing. Yet, I could also tell Coach didn't want to have to deal with this at the moment.

We had a game to play. I figured it was this guy's lucky day. Coach paid, and we parked.

This year the winner of the BB championship was West Union. Pelahatchie had lost their two best players, and their game play had fallen off.

West Union was a good team. They were a tall team. Coach said, though, that if we stopped their six-six big man, we would win it.

Our fans came out in droves. Focused and determined, we gave them something to see. I knew when Coach said they were a tall team, that we were going to press. Press, we did. We gave them fits. They may have been taller, but we were quicker. We ran them into the ground.

Levelheaded, Larry led the team under pressure while Rich and Jimmy were hot. Anything they threw up went into the basket. On the inside, Earl fought for every rebound. I got to go in for a couple of minutes, but the game was already in hand. We won by eleven.

After losing two years in a row in the semi-finals, we were going to the finals.

We enjoyed the moment but didn't take more than a few minutes to celebrate. Once we left the locker room, we were on to the next game.

"Done good," Coach said. "But we've got one more."

The guys and I went back to the hotel. We wanted to watch the next game to see who we were going to face, but it wasn't until later that night. Coach wanted us to rest up for the finals.

West Lauderdale, the A champ, was playing Forest Hill, the AA champ. Both teams were from the south division. I didn't know much about either team, but I knew by the time we played either team, Coach would.

So, we didn't worry about it. Yet in our room, Larry kept whispering to Virgil.

Laying across the bed, we were watching T.V. I sat up. "Okay, that's it. What's up? Don't tell me nothing."

Tilting his head, Mickey looked over at the two. He wanted the answer as well.

Larry was the honest sort. I don't think he even knew how to lie. He just shrugged.

"Not much," Larry said. "Virgil overheard Coach talking to his friend, Coach Tilman."

"Yeah," I pressed. "And?"

"They were just debating asking for a change in officials for our game tomorrow night."

Totally confused, I said, "I don't understand."

"Well," Larry began. "You remember that official at the State tournament, the one that kept making calls on us for anything?"

I nodded.

"He was set to be an official tomorrow night," Larry stated. "Coach didn't want that. He asked for a change."

"Seems the right thing to do. That guy had it in for us for no reason," I said.

"Hope so," Larry grimaced. "Just feels like the deck is stacked against us. I mean, we're going for the overall championship tomorrow night. We shouldn't have to worry about if we get a fair shake on the court. We have enough to worry about."

The room got quiet except for the T.V. I thought for a long moment.

"I think that Coach wouldn't want us to be concerned about it. He's always saying that we need to focus on our game. It's the only thing that we have control over. He'll take care of the rest. We're always facing long odds, all the time. Tomorrow night is no different."

Larry looked at me and then smiled. "When did you get to be so smart, Dean Barnes?"

"Just listen to what Coach says."

Ten minutes later, Ronnie, our manager, came in to ensure we were all set for lights out. We had a game to play the next day.

* * * *

Morning dawned but dragged on to what felt like forever.

Waiting and thinking drained my energy. The others were playing cards and walking around the hotel for the fifteenth time.

I was thinking. The previous year, I hadn't read any of the papers. I think I had just been overwhelmed with being there. This year after eating breakfast, I picked up the Clarion-Ledger. Turning to the sports section, I understood why reading the paper wasn't the best thing to do.

No one was giving us a chance. They made fun of us. They called us losers for not making it past Pelahatchie the last two years. I should give them credit that they did call us quick ball handlers and deadly shooters, but most of the article was on how Forest Hill was going to beat us.

Something about that just didn't sit right with me. The way I saw it, the Jackson paper thought we were a bunch of country hicks that didn't know the first thing about basketball, much less how to win.

Coach told us that we had accomplished the improbable winning three State titles in a row, but it seemed that no one in Jackson thought us good old boys should be in the tournament.

We had a team walk-through practice after breakfast. Like I knew he would, Coach had our game plan set. We had our assignments. We just had to do them.

Momma hadn't gotten to come down this year. I wished she had. I wanted her to be there if we won.

After practice, Rich told me that I should really appreciate this moment. He had wanted to win the state championship since he was old enough to dribble and to win the Grand Slam…that would be the icing of the cake.

"You guys have been winning so long, you take it for granted that you're going to win. For us that have been on the outside looking in, it wasn't that way. Facing New Site is like facing a mountain you can't climb."

I knew what Rich was saying. The Royals had a reputation, a well-earned reputation. We took the court to win, no matter if we were supposed to or not.

Finally, the call came to load up to go. It was time. We were leaving for the coliseum. Again, we rode in the same cars as we had the day before. Once more, Coach pulled into the parking lot right up to the booth where the same guy as yesterday held his hand out.

"Three cars, a dollar fifty."

Coach nodded and reached into his bag. He pulled out a paper bag. "There should be a hundred and fifty pennies there."

The guy frowned. "You don't have anything else?"

Shaking his head, Coach said, "Count 'em. Don't want to cheat you."

Releasing a sigh, the man didn't look like he wanted to count them. He was going to take them as is, but Coach refused to move. First count, the guy got a hundred and forty-eight pennies.

"I'm sure there's a hundred and fifty," Coach said. "Count them again."

Once again, the man counted a hundred and forty-eight. By this time, the line behind us was building. Glancing back, I couldn't see where it ended.

The attendant looked at Coach, then back at the bag of pennies. He handed them back to Coach.

"Just go."

"All three cars." Coach said, more as a statement than a question.

The man nodded.

"Thank you," Coach replied.

I don't think the guy wanted to see us again, but I can tell you that it made me feel pretty good. I never did like being treated like a second-class citizen. Apparently, neither did Coach.

There is no word to describe the feeling you have when you face your dream. It was one thing to envision what you wanted; it was another to face the reality of that dream.

For the first time, I was envious of the starters, even Larry. I wanted to play. Adrenaline flowed through my veins, but I understood what was expected of me. I had to be ready.

After I dressed, I fidgeted. I hated waiting.

Coach came in to talk, but I couldn't tell you what he said. A knock came on the door.

"Just play your game," Coach said.

Running out, I saw our fans standing and cheering. No one was sitting. The atmosphere was electric.

Glancing over at our opponents, I took a second look. Their horizontal striped uniforms and socks caught me off guard. They looked like they had escaped from prison except that they had numbers on the back.

I wouldn't have dared say a word to anyone about it. Coach would have had my head for making fun of a team.

Excitement at tip-off changed almost immediately. Forest Hill had gotten the ball first, but no sooner had we crossed centerline, when a whistle was blown. Rich had stepped in front of his man, who was cutting for the ball. The guy wasn't looking and ran Rich over.

Rich had done it a million times before. Usually, a foul was called. The official did make a call, but to all of our surprise, it was on Rich. It didn't get better from there.

Before the end of the first period, Rich had three fouls and so did Jimmy. In turn, I got my wish to play, but not the way I wanted to go into the game. We were fighting for our lives and needed both Rich and Jimmy.

Coach wouldn't let us complain about the officiating. We had a game to play. Our press wasn't working the way it had against West Union. We couldn't trap anyone without the whistle blowing.

There was no way to get in our groove scrambling and intercepting passes. To make things worse, Rich got his fourth foul in the third. With Rich out most of the game, our scoring would suffer.

Mid-way through the third, we fell flat and couldn't buy a bucket. We didn't give up, and we tied it with seven minutes in the fourth. Jimmy hit a couple of free throws.

This game, they weren't giving me a shot. I got called for traveling once when I double faked the guy on me and drove for an open lay-up. Larry threw the ball away when Jimmy got held on his cut down the lane.

Forest Hill pulled away by seven. Coach put Rich back into the game. We pulled back to within three points. Immediately, Rich hit an outside shot. As Rich ran back down the court out of the blue, he got called for his fifth foul.

Rich had fouled out, and he was followed closely by Jimmy. We never recovered and lost sixty-five to sixty.

The game left a bad taste in my mouth. In the locker room, Larry and I vented to each other. It had been quite obvious the officials weren't going to let us win.

"Don't go there."

I looked up from the bench to see Coach. He shook his head.

"If you do, you take away from what you accomplished," Coach said. "We have won three straight state championships. We made it to the finals—our little school came within a breath of winning it all."

"But, Coach," I said. "it's not fair."

Coach gave me a sad smile. "Don't expect anyone to give you breaks, Dean. You have to make them. We did our best. It's all we can do."

He released a long breath and turned back to everyone. "Hold your head high. You have done New Site proud."

With his head hanging down, Rich sat in silence. I felt bad for him. It was plain he was hurting. He had had a hot hand. He hadn't missed a shot he had taken during the game but hadn't been allowed to play, whether fair or not.

I guess that's how it was when you were competitive. Nothing felt right unless you won.

The next morning as we left the hotel, I grabbed a paper. The Jackson paper called the game sloppy. That I couldn't argue, but there was an unusual article. One of the fans of Forest Hill was quoted as saying New Site got cheated. *It was obvious that the officials weren't going to let New Site win.* The columnist said it was nothing more than being over-officiated. The fouls were about the same for both teams.

But I would have countered that Forest Hill's fouls didn't come at crucial times. They came when it made little difference: mainly, a few at the end of the half and end of the game when Forest Hill had the game in hand.

Reading on, I saw the column did acknowledge that the game was miserable because of the officiating. The officials called anything that looked like a potential violation. New Site wasn't allowed to get in a rhythm. For that matter, neither team could play their game, and both were great teams.

In the back seat, I crumbled up the paper. Frowning, I stared out the window.

Driving up the Natchez Trace, Coach looked back at me in the rear-view window. "Let it go. It's done."

Reckon Coach was right, but it gnawed at me something fierce. Championship games were a rare thing, but I saw the look in Coach's eyes. He had wanted it too.

Pressing my lips together tightly, I sighed. The only thing that calmed me was the fact that there was next year, and I knew that we were going to do everything we could to get back to that game.

1967-68 Season

Chapter Thirteen

Summer had just begun, and love was in the air. Not for me specifically, but it seemed that all the guys had girlfriends. Now, for some reason beyond my comprehension, they thought I needed one.

Virgil was dating one of the cheerleaders, Norma. She felt I should ask out her friend Ada May.

I knew Ada May. She was pretty enough, I supposed, with straight brown hair pulled back in a ponytail most days and large brown eyes. I mean, I knew all the girls that went to New Site since I started school.

Honestly, I hadn't thought much about her. Ada May was shy, and I don't think I had ever held a conversation with her. Despite that fact, Norma arranged it for me.

I'll tell ya I was a little excited. We were going to the drive-in, which was playing a James Bond movie with Sean Connery that I hadn't seen it yet.

After seeing an ad in one of Momma's magazines, I went out and bought some Old Spice aftershave. The bottle cost more than the movie we were seeing.

Virgil picked me up right after he did Norma. Then, we headed towards Ada May's place. It was on the way to the drive-in.

Out of all of us boys that played for Coach Carver, Virgil had the nicest car. He drove his dad's new red '67 Electra. It was nice. I discovered I loved that new car smell.

We never had a new one, even when we bought another car. Momma only got a used car, but it was new to us.

I didn't tell Momma or Grandma I had a date. Didn't want them to make more out of it than it was. Offering only the information that I would be back by ten thirty, I ran out the door.

No sooner than I got in the backseat, Virgil let out a loud hoot. "Whoo wee! Daggum, Dean, how much aftershave did you put on?"

"Not enough, it seems." I smiled, but my confidence fell about ten feet.

"Don't go making fun of Dean, Virgil," Norma said in a kind voice. "You're just not used to Dean wearing any…besides, it won't be as strong by the time we get to Ada May's."

"If you say so." Dean rolled down his window. "But I'm not taking any chances."

He gave me a smile. He didn't have to because I knew he was joking, but I suddenly felt uncomfortable, like maybe I shouldn't go.

It wasn't either of them. I liked them both. The two of them just clicked. The way they looked at each other when they thought no one else was looking, not to mention that Norma was a catch.

In my opinion, Norma was one of the prettiest girls in school. She was far and away the nicest. She'd talk to everyone. After a game, she always made a point to tell me I played a good game, whether I did or not. I considered Virgil and Norma a perfect couple.

There again, Virgil was what Larry called a go-getter. He had confidence around others that I envied.

I was much more comfortable on a basketball court or lost in my books. Girls were too confusing.

Norma gave me a smile. "I hope that Coach Carver doesn't do Ada May like he does me. Ada May is much too timid."

"What do you mean?"

She gave a look to Virgil and laughed. "Oh, you know, he's talked to me about being a distraction to poor Virgil here. Told me not to talk to other guys in the stands while he's playing a game."

"Coach knows that I'll take off into the stands," Virgil teased. "Can't have my girl flirting with another guy."

Swallowing hard, I knew that Coach didn't like distractions, but I didn't think he had to worry about me yet. It was only one date.

If I was nervous before, I was well beyond that when Virgil took a right turn down a long dirt road before getting to Ada May's, a brick ranch house with a barn out back. Her father was a farmer like most around here.

I got out of the car and went to the front door. Her mother answered the door and greeted me with a wide smile. When I walked inside, her father sat in a recliner in front of the T.V.

He looked up at me. "You guys had a good season last year. Do you think you can get number four?"

"Yes, sir," I answered truthfully. "That's our goal."

The next moment, Ada May walked out of the hallway. I found myself wishing I could have kept talking to her father about basketball.

Ada May looked real pretty. She had gotten her hair fixed up where it curled at the end and had put on some red lipstick. She wore a sleeveless pale blue shirt with a white sweater and tan pants.

"You ready?" I asked.

She nodded. "I'll be back before ten."

Holding the door, Ada May walked out. I followed her after I told her parents it was nice to meet them. Ada May didn't say a word but waited at the car for me to open her door. I did and then rounded the car to my door.

The girls talked until we got to Jack Sprats. We ate some hamburgers and then headed to the movie. I thought to myself things were going okay even though Ada May and I hadn't said two words to each other. We had spent our time talking to Virgil and Norma.

When we got to the drive-in, Virgil and I went to get popcorn and drinks for the girls. Virgil kinda ribbed me a little before we got back in the car. Then, the movie started.

Virgil settled back and put his arm around Norma. I thought for a long moment, and then decided I might try to do the same. After gathering up my courage, I looked over at her.

The poor thing was huddled against the door like I was about to maul her. Right then, it dawned on me that she didn't want to be here.

Leaning over, I whispered. "Doing Norma a favor?"

She hesitated for a long moment before nodding.

I smiled at her. "Me, too. Let's just enjoy the movie."

After that, I did just that, even though my mind wandered a great deal. I had to admit, I was a little disappointed. My first date wasn't going the way I thought it would. I had imagined that we would have at least talked a little, or maybe, I had thought she had wanted to be with me.

Deflated, I couldn't wait to get home. After Virgil dropped me off, I looked at the clock. Ten-ten. I wondered if anyone was at the gym to shoot around a bit. I changed and took Grandma's car up to the school.

The lights were on, but only Coach Carver's truck was parked out front. Walking in, I saw Coach sweeping the court.

"Too late to shoot around?" I asked.

Coach shook his head. "Na, but I might go ahead home. My wife is probably wondering where I'm at. Told her I was just running out to pick up some papers I left in my office. It's been over two hours…played a little ball while I was here. Do you mind locking up?"

I laughed to myself. Coach never let up when it came to basketball. School had just let out a week earlier for the summer, and he was already preparing for next year. It was common knowledge that Coach was always studying up on the game. Personally, I thought he already knew it all.

"Not at all. I won't be long. Just wanted to shoot."

"Larry and Rich left about fifteen minutes ago to get something to eat. They might come back. They didn't say." He walked over with broom in hand. Laying the handle against the wall, he looked at me. "Date didn't go so well?"

I frowned. Someone had run their mouth. There again, he always knew everything.

Coach gave me a knowing smile. "Wouldn't worry about it. We all have been there."

"Just don't understand girls, I reckon."

"Well, let me know when you do." He walked over and took a ball off the rack. Throwing it to me, he asked, "Do you want to play a little one-on-one?"

Of course, I did. Coach didn't mind playing us at all. We couldn't beat him, but we tried. Wasn't no more than ten minutes passed when Rich and Larry walked onto the court. Mickey followed closed behind them. They had driven by and seen my car.

Coach left shortly after, but we played on well after midnight. It wasn't such a bad night, after all.

* * * *

The sound of the basketball bouncing echoed in the gym. The ball bounced against the rim, rebounded by a pair of strong hands, and immediately put through the net.

I took it on one bounce and passed it to Rich. "Your ball."

Rich dribbled at the point for a minute until everyone was set. He started toward Larry, pivoted to his left with a quick step unleashed a jumper. Swish. The ball slid through without touching the rim.

"That's a win," Rich smiled mischievously.

A whistle blew. Coach Carver clapped his hands. I sucked in air. Even though we had been playing around together all summer, our organized practices were about to begin with the start of school.

"Let's get started. New year. New season. Old goal. We have three State championships. Make no doubt about it. We're going for four. We aren't going to sit on our laurels.

"The road before us is tougher than it's ever been. We have a large target on our backs. Everyone wants to take us down. We are going to work harder, train harder to get ready for the season.

"We know what we have to do. Let's go do it."

As we gathered around Coach's blackboard, Mickey leaned in to me.

"What's a laurel?"

I wanted to chuckle, but he was serious. Instead, I whispered, "Our achievements. He doesn't want us to be content with our past. He wants us to look to the future."

Coach must have heard. He smiled at me and nodded.

For a moment, I studied Coach Carver. I had run into Donnie over the summer out at Booneville. He was going to Northeast but was working moving timber during school break.

We talked about basketball, but before he left, he gave me some advice.

"Trust Coach," Donnie said. "There's not a better one out there."

Simple words, but I understood what he was saying. It was just going to be hard. I wanted to be a starter this year. We only had two seniors last year which meant there were three of us juniors fighting for two positions, Virgil, Mickey, and me.

Coach had a way of separating being a friend and coach. There was no question who he was. Among us boys, his leadership was never challenged. He treated us fairly and pulled us together as a team.

He taught us how to play ball: shoot, play defense, and get into shape. He knew basketball better than anyone. If we were having a problem in a game, he would call a quick time-out, and he would have an answer for us.

Now, in practices, Coach was hard on us, but we knew it was to prepare us for the game. He taught us how to win.

After going over what we were going to do that day in practice, we broke into two groups. Most of what we were going over wasn't new, but it would be how we executed it this year.

We had a few new boys moving up from the B-team, including Roy Turner and Billy Reed. Both were sophomores. I liked Roy a lot. He always hustled.

I'll be honest. It felt good to practice. I didn't even dread the blasted whistle that signaled practice had come to an end, and running was about to begin. From the corner of my eye, I saw Ronnie with a stopwatch in one hand and pencil and pad in the other.

Coach took to the sidelines and turned to his manager. "You ready?"

"Yes, sir," Ronnie answered with a smile. I think everyone felt pretty good that things were back to normal.

Scratching his head as we positioned ourselves on the line, Coach said, "I've been thinking about this a lot, but for the life of me, I can't figure out who's the fastest on the team. What do you think, boys? Do you think it's Rich? Or maybe Larry at the far end? Betcha' it's Dean there. Why are you shaking your head, Virgil? Don't think so?"

We began shouting out names. I said JC because I didn't want to say myself. But I thought I was pretty fast. No one could agree who was the fastest.

"Well, I think the only fair thing would be a race. You guys up to it?"

"Yeah! Let's go!" J.C. playfully shouted. "I'm ready for everyone to eat my dust."

"Ain't gonna happen," Virgil said. "You're gonna be able to see me beat you because you're gonna be behind me."

Eagerly, we all readied. Coach blew the whistle, and we were off like a bunch of hooligans. With every bit of energy we had, we ran hard. I couldn't even tell you who was beside me. I was stretching out to win.

Crossing the line, I collapsed beside the wall along with most everyone else. Looking up, I saw Coach turn to Ronnie.

"Did you get the time?"

"Yes, sir. Thirty-three seconds." Ronnie wrote on his pad.

The hullabaloo of the race quieted into silence. All eyes fixed on Coach. He sat twirling his whistle in his hand with a smile like a cat that just swallowed the canary.

"Guys, we've been had," Rich said as he caught his breath.

Crawling back to my feet, I had to laugh to myself. Coach got us good. There wouldn't be any lagging behind running this year.

Then out of the silence, Mickey asked, "But who won?"

Chapter Fourteen

We started the year with a dominating victory over Houlka but turned around and barely beat Myrtle. Then we settled into a rhythm.

The papers called us a force, especially our defense. We had a devastating three-quarter press and our notorious one-two-two full-court press.

Mickey and I had been rotating in and out of the starting rotation, depending on who we were playing. Me not starting all the time hadn't sat well with Momma.

"You're a junior," she said. "Troy started when he was a sophomore."

"Momma, please don't go say nothing," I pleaded. "I'm not as good as Troy was."

"You play a different position," she pointed out. "You've got a great shot."

It was exasperating. I loved my momma, but Lord have mercy on me, she was stubborn. Grandma even tried to talk Momma out of interfering.

"Nothing good ever comes with trying to influence a coach, not that you could with Coach Carver," Grandma said. "Coach has been right good to Dean here. Don't ya go getting him mad at the boy."

Momma still ranted. Before she could go and do something stupid, I went to Missy. Thank goodness Missy was able to talk Momma off a cliff.

"She just loves you," Missy said.

I didn't retort that I thought it was more that Momma was embarrassed that as a junior, I wasn't a starter. Momma didn't understand the way the Royals did things. More importantly, I was part of this *dynasty*. I had played on two State championship teams.

Besides, I had faith in Coach. We won or lost as a team. If he thought I deserved to play, he would play me. That was just the way I felt.

Not that I didn't want to play. I did. Moreover, I worked hard every day to prove I was ready to play whenever he called on me.

Coach had us prepared for every game. Going into the Baldwyn High School Invitational Basketball Tournament, we were undefeated, having won our first ten games. The tournament only invited the best teams to play.

Excitement was in the air. We were finally getting our shot at Tupelo in the semi-finals.

Tupelo was the largest school in the North. The AA school had won the overall title in both '65 and '66. We had never played them before because they had refused to play us.

Most times, Momma only went to the home games, but for this one, I had specially called Missy and asked if she would take Momma. Missy said she was going anyway, and it wouldn't be a problem.

God love her. She had become a good friend to me. Over the last few years, she had made my life easier, helping out with Grandma. When Momma wasn't around, she would come and sit with Grandma while I practiced or even went out with my friends. She would laugh and say she was a mean checkers player now.

"Leave early," I warned her. "Won't get a seat otherwise. It won't work if you leave at the last minute with the expectation of getting inside the gym."

"Don't you worry none," Missy said. "You go and beat 'em."

Pulling into the parking lot at Baldwyn, I felt more than ready to play. Coach had told me at practice that morning that I would be starting. I could feel the adrenaline flowing. When I got off the bus in my red leather letter jacket, I felt a wave of pride sweeping through me as I walked alongside my teammates into the gym.

I had just passed an older man with a thinning hairline at the ticket table. Dressed in a tweed jacket, he raised his hand and stopped Roy. "You have to pay."

Roy looked at me, confused but reached in his pocket. I shook my head.

"Coach, they're trying to make Roy pay," I yelled.

I didn't have to say it a second time. Coach barreled back to the ticket table.

"Is there a problem? This kid is part of my team, the New Site Royals. We're playing in an hour," Coach said in a calm voice, but his eyes told a different story.

The man pushed back his glasses on his nose with his finger. "I know you're the Royals, Coach, but you have too many players. We have rules to follow. The rules state ten players and one manager get in free. The rest have to pay. That's all…and if that's your second manager over there, he has to pay, too."

Standing beside Coach, I saw Ronnie with a bag of balls in his hand. He just shrugged.

Coach grimaced. "I don't think so. There are twelve Royals and two managers."

The man sighed. "I'm sorry. I have no control over the matter. I just follow the rules." He glanced behind Coach and waved his hand toward the long line. "Look, just pay for three and go inside."

"Here, Coach," Roy pulled out a dollar. "I don't mind."

"I do," Coach said. "Put it back." He took a deep breath before he gestured to all of us. "Back on the bus, boys. We're going home."

Without a sound, we pivoted like an army detachment and walked back toward the bus. Coach followed.

Glancing back over my shoulder, I saw the man in the tweed coat almost knock over the table to catch up to Coach. He yelled, "Where are you going? You can't just leave. You have a game to play."

Abruptly, Coach wheeled around. "We can't play as a team if we aren't allowed inside. We are a team—all of us. If we can't get inside together, then we all go home."

I was taken back by the intensity in his voice. I realized we had two players that rotated their uniforms to be on the team that hardly ever got into a game, but it was the way Coach was. If someone was willing to work hard to be on the team, he was on the team.

Behind the man in the tweed jacket, Baldwyn's principal came running out. "It's all right, Mr. Johnson," he addressed the man. "Go back to the table. I'll take care of things." Circling back to Coach, he smiled. "Sorry about that, Coach Carver. A misunderstanding. Of course, your players don't have to pay. Just make your way back inside…all of you."

I exchanged a smile with Larry. We walked in together, the New Site Royals.

Dressed and ready to take the court, Coach held the handle of the locker room's door. "Let's go play ball, boys. Show them who the New Site Royals are."

He opened the door. I had never been so focused as I was when we burst out on the court. I didn't even see the crowd. I only saw the court, my teammates, my opponents, and the orange ball.

From tip-off, we hit the court hard. It didn't matter that we faced the number one ranked team in the state. We played like we had practiced.

We played a man-to-man, switching off immediately when they made a pick. Rich was red-hot and couldn't miss. Larry read their defense readily enough. I even had a couple of good shots along with Virgil. We were leading by four at halftime.

Coach made a few adjustments. We came out and hit them with our press. I played on the left side of the one-two-two press. Larry and I trapped them in the corner. They kept throwing it away for us to steal or passing it out of bounds.

Rich couldn't be stopped. Neither could I. With the press, we kept getting turnovers that led to lay-ups. I was on the receiving end of those giveaways and kept making shots from the wing, one that banked off the backboard and dropped for two. Leading by twenty-four in the fourth, Coach relieved us starters.

By the end of the game, Coach had cleared the bench. We ended up winning by twenty-one.

I have to say I felt pretty good. It was the first time I had scored more than twenty, ending up with twenty-two. Couldn't compare to Rich, though. He had thirty.

The next night, we took the Baldwyn tournament by downing the standout team, Baldwyn. Rich again led the scoring with twenty-three, but Virgil and JC followed this time with seventeen and fifteen, respectively. Larry ate them up with assists, hitting just the right man for the shot.

In the tournament's deciding game, I didn't break double digits but was elated. Taking pride in my defense with my foot work and quick hands, I had three takeaways at crucial times in our four-point win.

As we left with the trophy, no one questioned that we were a contending team for the best in the state, but more importantly, we left with the belief that no one could stop us.

* * * *

There was nothing but basketball.

We took our undefeated record into the County Tournament and won. Each night we took the court, we faced an opponent that wanted nothing more than to take us down.

After Christmas, our record was blemished after we traveled into Corinth. We lost by two. The ball just didn't roll our way.

Coach said to pick our heads up. We had more games to play. "We'll get back when they come to our house. Focus on our next game."

Our next game was in the Belmont Tournament. We won two straight, taking us to the finals against the home team, Belmont.

Saturday night came, and I guess you could say we walked into a hostile environment. Belmont fans were at us the second we took the court for warm-ups. I shrugged it off. We had played better teams. I expected we would win this one easily enough.

Coach gave me the opportunity to start this game. I was feeling pretty good about myself as Larry and I exchanged a laugh before tip-off. The official heaved the ball upward and J.C. hit it over to me. For some unknown reason, the ball slipped through my fingers into a Belmont player's hand.

The gym erupted on my mistake. Can't say the night got any better for me. I seemed to be flat-footed and a step behind my man, and I couldn't buy a bucket. To make matters worse, I missed my free throws. I never missed free throws.

Coach sat me down at the beginning of the second quarter. The game was nip and tuck. The Royals led by two when Larry passed it toward Rich, but it didn't last. The ball was intercepted, and Belmont scored an easy two with a lay-up. Not to mention, calls weren't going our way.

Seconds ticked down in the half, and we had fell behind. Larry grimaced as he took the ball from J.C.'s inbound pass. With great defense from Belmont, he didn't get the ball over half court when time ran out. At half, we were losing by eight.

Coach wiped his forehead and stared at us for a long moment. No doubt about it, Coach was angry.

"If you're not ready to play, you can't just turn it on."

His voice resonated through me. He ranted at what each of us was doing wrong. Then, he took a deep breath. "Now, listen up. This is what we are going to do to win."

Coach put me back into the game. I might not have had my shot tonight, but I didn't need it for defense. At times, I felt like one of those hamsters that kept running on their wheel and got nowhere, but I didn't stop.

When the final buzzer rang, I looked up at the scoreboard. We were tied.

We were going to overtime, and it was a catfight. As we trailed by two in the final seconds of the second overtime, Virgil hit a bucket extending the game for a third overtime.

Within seconds of the third overtime, Rich was called for a foul. It was his fifth. He was out of the game.

His face fell, and he stood motionless. Larry went over to Rich.

"Don't worry. We'll get them."

On the front end of the one and one, Belmont hit the front edge of the basket but the ball circled, fell backward and down through the net on the first shot but missed the second free throw.

The game carried on as we fell behind by three. With the clock running down, Virgil barreled down the court and was fouled.

I looked up at the clock. There were only eleven seconds left. Virgil went to the line, hitting the first one. Coach called a time-out.

Huddling close, Coach looked over his shoulder at the clock, then back at us.

"Eleven seconds. We're not out of this. When Virgil hits this free-throw, Larry needs to foul the Brown kid before any more time runs off the clock. Push him. Whatever you have to do to make sure the official sees you. He's their worst free-throw shooter. Block out and rebound that ball and get it to Virgil. Let's pull this thing out."

Lining up at the line, Larry set up beside Brown. Virgil swished the free throw. I looked over at Larry, expecting him to foul, but he moved back on defense. Glancing over at Coach, he was livid, screaming at Larry.

Then, it dawned on Larry that he was supposed to foul, but it was too late. Time ran out. Belmont won.

The stands exploded.

Standing mid-court, I was dumbfounded. Over at the bench, Coach released his frustration. He launched his red towel high into the air. So high it caught in the rafter.

I guess I was kinda in shock, leaving the court. We were supposed to have beat Belmont handily. I walked into the locker room. The first thing I saw was Larry on the bench with his head hung down. He looked like a dog who got caught raiding the chicken coop.

"Sorry, Coach," Larry began when Coach came into the room. "I don't know why I blew my assignment. I don't know where my head was."

"It's over. One play didn't cost us the game," Coach said. "This is one we can learn from, but remember, we can't make mental mistakes in the state tournament where it would make a difference. That goes for all of you. We didn't come to play tonight."

Getting dressed, I buttoned up my shirt and grabbed my gym bag. Looking over at Larry, he hadn't even taken off his uniform.

"Come on, buddy," I said. "The bus is waiting."

He sighed. "Yeah, I guess."

"Look, you didn't lose it for us. Like Coach said, we're a team. I know it's hard when you make the first mistake of your life, but you'll survive. Take it from someone who has made plenty."

A small smile emerged at my joke. We walked out together. Up above us, Coach's towel hung. No one had taken it down.

* * * *

The next morning was Saturday, and I got up early. Practice was at nine, but I hadn't slept much anyway. When you lose a game you should have won, it eats at you.

Yet it could have been the fact I knew what was going to happen when I got to the gym. We had one of these practices last year after a similar loss.

I tied my laces tight. The whistle blew. Glancing over at my teammates, we all took a deep breath and took the court. We were still going strong at one in the afternoon. Coach hadn't let up.

"Run it again."

Willing my body to move into position, I crouched in a defensive position. We were running our half-court press. Larry threw the ball to Roy, who was taking it down against us.

Roy threw it over to Billy Reed and Larry and Rich converged on him. Billy threw it back to Roy, where I picked him up. From the corner of my eye, I saw Billy cut through the middle and barrel over Rich. Crawling back to his feet, Billy headed toward the locker room.

"Where do you think you're going, Mr. Reed?" Coach asked with his whistle in hand.

"Well, Coach," Billy explained. "The way I got it figured that's my fifth foul. I'm out."

Billy was still running when I left.

* * * *

Walking into the house, I saw Missy at the kitchen table with Grandma. They had clippings spread all over the table.

I picked up a few from the *Banner Independent* and *Tupelo Journal*. They all were from this season.

New Site Lays Claim to Prentiss County Laurels. We had beaten Baldwyn again to claim the title. We had lost to them at the end of the season over at Baldwyn during one of our last regular-season games.

New Site Defends District Honors. We defeated our county rival, Wheeler. Since not only the first place team advanced, but also the second place team, Wheeler moved on to North Half. Again, we beat them for the North Half crown, but not until coming close playing Randolph.

New Site Makes an Unprecedented Fourth Straight Trip to the Tournament of Champions. In Morton, we took the State B title. Beating Burns and Improve pretty easily, we had a hard-fought game against West Lincoln. We ended up winning by five.

History Was Made. New Site Returns Again. The article was about our consecutive wins in the state tournament. Over the years, we had won our championships by winning every game. We had placed only first along the way.

Winning State had become an expectation around here.

We were hitting the road down to Jackson in the morning, and we had our own expectation: to win the Grand Slam.

I had a man ask me after winning the State again how we did it. I told him what Coach told us. *Take one game at a time.* I didn't add that I thought it was the way we played as a team. We had come through every obstacle and survived the pressure together.

Larry was coming over first thing the next day to pick me up. Once again, we were driving down in cars. Once more, Larry and I were riding with Coach.

"Whatcha doing?" I asked, laying the clippings down.

Missy smiled real big at me. "Do you have to ask? Your Grandma and I are putting together your scrapbook for this year."

"What?" My eyebrows rose. "For me?"

Grandma tapped my arm when I bent down and gave her a hug. "I can't take all the credit. Missy here has been the driving force making sure we get the right newspaper articles."

I sat down with them and flipped through the pages they had already completed. For a long moment, I couldn't say anything. It went back to when I was a freshman.

As if reading my mind, Missy said, "It's our way to tell you we wish we could be with you this weekend. I feel really bad I can't make it down there."

"It's fine," I replied. I certainly understood Grandma not being able to go, not with her health.

Momma had said she would go if we made it back this year, but she didn't. Momma said it was because we couldn't afford it. I thought it was more that Missy couldn't come. At least, they had made it to the State title game.

Missy had started at Northeast last fall. She was going to be a nurse and couldn't get out of a test coming up on Friday.

I felt a little sad. I wanted them there to see us win because I made up my mind that was what we were going to do—win it all.

* * * *

It felt like home.

Coming back to Jackson, we stayed at the same Sun-'n-Sand Motel as we always did. IHOP was exactly where we had left it and still had the best pancakes and sausage ever.

We had come down the Thursday before we were to play on Friday. To get to where I wanted, we had to get through the semi-final game against Lloyd Star, the BB

State champ. Lying down for the night, I couldn't get to sleep.

Coach's words echoed in my head. *Take one game at a time.* Lloyd Star was from the South. I didn't know anything about them except what Coach had told us.

"They've got one guy that's a tremendous ballplayer. They call him Moochie. We are going to try and shut him down, but the key is closing in, doubling up on guarding the others. Blocking them from passing the ball to Moochie. Keep the ball away from Moochie."

This year, I was rooming with Rich, Larry, and Mickey. I rolled over on my side and surprisingly stared straight into Rich's eyes. He was awake.

"You need to sleep," he said.

I thought for a moment of telling him he should too, but then I thought better about it. Rich had that serious look on his face. Kinda reminded me of Coach.

"Thinking about the game."

He gave me a nod. "Don't worry about anything. Play like we practiced."

I was silent for a time. "Do you think we can do it this year?"

A smile crossed his face, taking me by surprise. Rich never smiled. "Yeah, I do."

"Me, too."

"Good," he said. "Now, go to sleep."

It was a restless sleep. I wanted it to be game time. I wanted to play.

Coach had told me I was going to start. I kept going over my assignments in my mind, knowing I would be battling a big guy. I would be the tallest Royal to take the court to start the game. We had been here before, but the truth was, I had butterflies.

I wanted to win this, not really for myself, but for the guys, for Momma and Grandma, for the community…for

Coach. I couldn't get it out of my head that I wanted to make Troy proud.

Taking the court the next afternoon, I played with my heart and attacked. With Coach starting a much shorter line-up than Lloyd Star, we had to scrap for every score and pester them into making errant passes. I battled down under the net for rebounds.

There were times going into games when it had just felt right. It was one of those games. Everything just clicked. Early in the game, that Moochie guy tied up the game seven to seven, but Rich came back down the court. After being fouled, he hit two free throws. We didn't look back.

There was a point after the half when Lloyd Star tried to mount a comeback. They began double-teaming Rich, but Larry passed me the ball on the left side, their weak side, and I sank three shots in a row. For that matter, when Larry got fouled, he stepped confidently to the line and hit his free throws. Virgil stepped up, which was amazing since he had been so sick the previous night.

By the time the final buzzer rang, I had spent every bit of energy I had and was totally exhausted. I had scored sixteen points, not that it could compare to Rich's thirty-five, but I had pulled down ten rebounds. Ten tough hard fought rebounds.

We had won; we didn't bother to celebrate. We had our eyes on the next game.

This is what we had come for—the overall championship. This was our chance because, at the end of the next game, we would have our opponent, Tupelo, the team we had blown out earlier in the year.

* * * *

I should have been exhausted, but I wasn't. Larry, Rich, Mickey, and I had just finished another hand of cards when Ronnie knocked on our door with the official news it was Tupelo.

The news had been expected. We were in for a battle the following night.

We had beaten Tupelo easily in the Baldwyn Tournament, but no one on our team thought this was going to be a cakewalk. Tupelo wasn't the same team they had been the last time we played them.

Mid-season, they had changed coaches. To me, though, it was the fact they had three new players, one of whom Coach said was real good. I found out Coach wanted me to take him. I was going to start again; Rich told me.

I think that Coach had talked over the scenarios with Rich. That, or Rich overheard his talking. Rich said he thought we were going to be hit with a press.

Rich was talking in-depth to Larry. I think the two of them went over the game almost as much as Coach. Honestly, I was still riding the high of the victory that afternoon. Besides, I had faith in Coach.

I could hear Coach now. *This is a different team than the one we played.* I don't think he had to worry about us taking it for granted. This game meant too much to us.

For the first time since I'd known Rich, he seemed nervous. I didn't think he was going to get much sleep that night either. Larry looked dead serious, too.

I got ready for bed. We would be up early to prepare. I expected that Coach wouldn't get any sleep, either. He would be up all night going over the scouting reports and coming up with a game plan.

Pulling the covers up around me, I needed sleep. My body ached. I had taken a beating under the basket, but it mattered little. I wasn't going to let a few bruises slow me down.

For one night, I would dream. The next day, I would make that dream a reality.

* * * *

The morning dawned.

I woke up with one thought. I didn't even taste the pancakes but read the paper. The guys told me to put it down. They just didn't know I wasn't reading about us, but Tupelo.

Well, I guess I had read about us first...about Coach. It was the first time I had seen someone give Coach the acknowledgment of how good he was outside our community. The writer talked about how Coach was never satisfied and was always looking for that something extra to help us win. Coach was always coming up with a new play and usually with an attack to win the game. The paper called Coach one of the greatest.

What else could you say about a Coach that had taken a team with only three wins in two years, and made them into a dynasty? He had come from coaching a AA school to coaching us, a bunch of farmer boys. Guess you could call us good ol' boys.

Glancing over my shoulder, I saw Coach in the booth across from us. He was in deep discussion with his friend, Coach Tilman from Tishomingo. To his side, Coach's wife sat quietly.

She never said much, but she caught my eye as I was looking. She gave me a kind smile. Something told me that even she wanted this as badly as we did for him. Coach deserved this.

I went back to reading. This year, the papers were giving us a chance. They weren't simply dismissing us as a fluke.

All of us boys wanted it, but there was no doubt, Rich wanted it bad. He had a strong desire to win. I could never remember him playing a bad game. Every time he took to the court, he gave a hundred and ten percent and accepted nothing less from us. I found myself wanting it for him too.

My desire to gain this title strengthened; my confidence grew. Drinking down my orange juice, I knew we had only one obstacle in front of us.

* * * *

Waiting to run onto the court, I felt my heart pound; my palms sweated.

Coach had given us our assignments. There was nothing left to do but play.

I took one deep breath and ran behind Virgil. Breaking into two lines, we began our lay-ups. After laying one in, I took my place to rebound. I stared at our opponents.

For the first time in my life, I would be playing against a black player. Coach said he was the one that had made the difference in Tupelo's play. Hank Busing was tough, and he was mine to handle.

I could feel the anticipation in the air at opening tip-off. *This is our year,* I told myself as the official threw up the jump ball.

Tupelo got the opening tip-off. Immediately, Busing had the ball and dribbled down the court. Running to get into position, I barely crouched before the guy did a hesitation dribble and went around me. He passed it over to their big guy who hit the opening two.

Dang. The guy was quick. I took the ball out to throw it in to Larry. Immediately, Tupelo hit us with a press. We had prepared, and we lined up at the free-throw line and broke in different directions to spread the floor. Seeing Larry open, I passed it toward him. Busing picked it off and threw it over to an open teammate in the corner for another two.

Taking it again, I got it in to Virgil, but as soon as I did, Busing stole the ball from Virgil and once again hustled over half court, laid it up, making another two points. laid it up. We were losing six to nothing before we had even gotten the ball down court.

Coach called time out and told us to do another breakout play. "Just nerves. Calm down. Play your game."

Coming out of the huddle, we fought back. We got on the board when J.C. hit a couple of free throws. Then,

Busing came down and hit another two. Even when he missed, Tupelo would rebound it and put it up. They were all over us.

Larry hit a shot from the point. On the throw-in, Rich intercepted the ball and nailed a jumper. At the end of the quarter, we were losing fifteen to twelve. Coming back out in the second, we crawled to a lead when J.C. hit another couple of free-throws.

We were in a battle, but I felt lead-footed against this Busing kid. I had never played against anyone as quick and agile. I couldn't stop him. And on offense, I couldn't get a shot off. Busing was in my face. I couldn't even get the ball.

Moreover, each time I was throwing the ball in against their press, they moved their big guy in front of me. I couldn't see around him, and if I got it off, they had Busing there to pick the pass off.

After their last score, I took the ball and slapped it. The boys broke and spread the floor, but I couldn't see anyone open. All I saw were blue uniforms. The official stood to my side, counting. Four...three...two...

I reared back and threw the ball down the court. I didn't know who would get it but figured it would be better than giving the ball back to them under their basket. The look on Larry's face told of his total shock.

Tupelo got the ball and came down, scoring again. We were losing by nine at the half.

In the locker room, Coach wasn't mad, but tried to refocus us. *Execute better. Hit the open man.*

I wanted to say I was trying. Looking at Coach, I wanted him to take me out. He gave me a lock to tell me that wasn't happening.

"Do your best," Coach said. "The game isn't over."

Rich couldn't miss. His game seemed to have gone to another level, but we couldn't stop them on defense. We couldn't get in sync. They seemed to be a step in front of us, especially with the Busing guy whizzing around us.

Coach had pulled me from guarding Busing, but Rich didn't have much luck either. The guy was the fastest player we had ever played against. He would be in a position one second and gone in a blink of an eye to the other side of the court while we would still be standing there.

We didn't give up and pulled to within six points late in the third. It was the closest we ever got. With less than a minute to go, the game had already been decided. Coach looked dejected on the bench. It cut me to the quick.

Tupelo won by eleven.

I was devastated. My heart sank. We had lost again. *It was impossible. We couldn't have lost again.*

Around me, the world became a blur. Everyone's family surrounded them, comforting them as best they could. I stood alone with an overwhelming feeling to cry, something I could never do.

Last year, I had watched Forest Hill take the title and had sworn to get back here. *All that hard work, sweat, and sacrifice for nothing!*

I didn't know what to do. *Go to the locker room. Stand here and look like an idiot.* I felt lost.

Suddenly, I felt a hand on my shoulder. It was Coach. The disappointment in Coach's face had vanished.

"Come on, boy," Coach said. "Let's get the hell out of here."

Not even looking back, I headed toward the locker room. I wanted to tell Coach I was sorry. My mouth opened, but Coach shook his head.

He read my pain. "No need for overthinking. It's life. Sometimes you win. Sometimes you don't. We just played a better team tonight."

Behind us, the guys followed us inside. We got dressed in silence. Coach said nothing until everyone was ready.

Coach pressed his lips tightly together as if it was hard for him to say. Finally, though, he found the words.

"I can't tell you guys how proud I am of you… all of you. Don't let this take away from what you accomplished this year. You won State for four years straight." He took a deep breath. "You might ask yourself, how do you accept this loss? By remembering that you did the best you could. There is nothing to regret if you try your best. It was all I asked. Hold your head high."

Coach meant it. I saw it in his eyes. I wished it was that easy to feel better.

I sighed and picked up my bag. This one hurt. It was going to take a long time to get over…if ever.

Chapter Fifteen

We guys had been devastated after losing the big game despite Coach telling us how much we had to be proud of. I mean, we had just won our fourth State title. Why did I feel like we had failed? Afterward, I had gone off by myself and found a secluded spot on one of the flights of stairs in the back of the hotel.

I sat in silence, reliving every moment of the game. I winced thinking of the ball I looped so high. I had wished with everything in me I could take that back and find a way to get the ball to Larry. I felt I let the team down.

Losing track of time, I had heard footsteps walking toward the stairs. At first, I thought I would have to move, but they stopped at the railing.

Immediately, I recognized voices—Coach Carver and Rich.

"Coach," Rich began. "I'm glad to have found you. I couldn't sleep either."

"Shouldn't let it get to you. You guys did all you could do. I couldn't have asked any more from you and the team."

"I know. I know what you told us…winning four in a row. Two years in a row in the finals, but I would be lying if I didn't say this one left a bad taste in my mouth."

"It's because you're competitive. It's the way we're made. If we play a game, we expect to win, but honestly, I couldn't have been prouder. We did our best… it's all that we can do."

There was a long silence.

"Coach, thank you for letting me be a part of this. I hafta tell you about the first time I saw you. Must have been in the sixth or seventh grade. I got to go to see Booneville when they were the powerhouse.

"No one thought you could win. All the odds were against it, but you couldn't tell it looking at you or the Royals. There was something about watching you that I knew I wanted to be part of it. I was so excited when Dad got a job so we could move to New Site.

"I have never cared about anything but playing ball. I've gone through school without a nickel in my pocket, but… I couldn't have been happier. I got to play for you. Thank you…I just wanted to be a winner."

"You always have been."

The words hung in the air.

At first, I thought Coach was talking about how good Rich was. I mean, the guy was intense and focused, and one of the best shots around.

But that night, it was dawning on me that it meant more.

* * * *

Out in the gym one day after school, I sat there staring at the empty court. Rich walked up to me. We talked for a couple of hours about the season.

"It was a tough one, but I was thinking about Lloyd Star game. You remember when you picked off the pass and had that guy…number…who was it… number twenty-three. The look on the guy's face…I thought he was going to tackle you," Rich said.

"Not like the look on your face when you fouled out of the Belmont game," I teased. "There was poor Larry telling you we had it…we didn't. Coach got so mad he sent his towel into the rafters."

The memory brought a smile to Rich. "Hear they aren't taking it down. Their moment of glory, I guess."

"Let them have it. We have ours." I shrugged. "We had a damn good year."

"The Royals have had four damn good years," Rich said. "I might not have been here for but two of them, but not a bad legacy to leave behind."

A moment later, we were shooting around. Larry and Mickey joined us not long after, then Roy followed.

Rich had the look Troy had had, a resolve to prove his worth to the world. Troy would have done it, too, if given a chance. I felt sure Rich would. He was going to play at Northeast, but I thought he should have gone D1.

Guess them college coaches weren't looking for heart, 'cause to me there wasn't a better player around than Rich. He had what Coach called the ability to win no matter the odds.

Troy had had that drive too.

A sudden clarity surged through me about the difference between other teams and us, besides Coach Carver. Winning to us wasn't just stepping on the court. It was all of us stepping on the court...together.

Season 1968-69

Chapter Sixteen

Under a blanket of brilliant stars, I sat on the porch. Momma had gone out and hadn't gotten home, but Grandma was sleeping. She hadn't felt good lately, and I worried about her.

I worried about a lot of things. I guess it was just the way I was.

School was going to be out the following week. I would be a senior come fall. For some reason, it bothered me. I reckoned I had been thinking of Troy a lot lately and wondered what he would have thought about our streak that he started.

He had loved playing basketball. Yet, I couldn't shake the memory that his basketball career had ended after winning the State championship.

The thought depressed me. The truth of the matter was, I realized that my ball days would be over at the end of the season. Then where would I be? I had never thought of my future beyond high school or basketball.

Amid the stars in the night sky, I looked up, closed my eyes, and prayed. I had gotten that feeling in my stomach, the one that doesn't last long, that makes you feel insignificant and small. I supposed it was the realization that I'm only one of a billion people on this earth.

I couldn't dismiss the question—who was I?

My senior year promised to be disappointing. I doubted Coach was going to let up on us. It was going to be another hard year...working toward what? We had already done the impossible. Didn't think winning the overall title would ever be within our grasp again.

Suddenly, across the clear sky, a shooting star fell. Just like that, in a blink of an eye, I had a wish. Grandma had told me that when I was knee-high to a grasshopper. I didn't believe in that foolishness anymore, but I made the wish anyway.

Please give us one more shot.

Boy, would Troy have laughed at me. Staring in the dark, I imagined life as it had been, Troy playing ball with me out back of our old house. I would get so mad when he beat me, and he always beat me. Then, Troy would taunt me until we would play again. Thinking about it now, I realized he wouldn't let me go back inside until Dad had drunk enough to pass out.

Strange because at that moment, the memory didn't conjure up resentment toward my Dad, but made me smile thinking of Troy—my older, protective brother.

I could hear Troy now. *What is wrong with you, boy? Feeling sorry for yourself because you came in second in the state for two consecutive years. Oughtta be happy. You have everything in front of you. Just like you can't be afraid to lose, you can't be scared to live.*

Then I realized I had gone off the deep end. I had Troy sounding like Coach Carver.

There I sat in the dark with my memories, good memories...comforting memories.

* * * *

Coach Carver took out his 12-gauge shotgun and loaded two shells in the chamber. He filled his vest with enough cartridges to last during the hunt. He whistled.

Over my shoulder, I saw two of Coach's bird dogs leap off the truck. The dogs were lean and well-muscled. One had brown spots on its coat; the other was mostly white.

Walking over the dew-covered field, I carried my gun up on my shoulder with the quail bag attached to my belt. We were heading for the tall grass of an uncut field.

It was the second time since school ended that I had gone out with Coach. I found myself becoming a pretty good hunter. I discovered hunting was a way to release any pent-up frustrations, not that I thought Coach had any. I just knew I did.

The previous week, Grandma had gotten out of the hospital. She had had an incident where her glucose went up too high and went into some crisis where she had trouble breathing and was confused. Thankfully, they got it under control. She was home and doing better than she had for a long while.

It was Momma I was feeling a little worried about, or maybe it was just me. She had been dating a man from church, Harold Lyndsey. She hadn't said much about him to me, but after Grandma got home from the hospital, Momma said she was gonna marry the guy.

Reckoned she was happy about it and wanted me to be. It had been a long while since Dad died and all. I really didn't know why it bothered me, except I didn't like the guy much.

Mr. Lyndsey had been married before, but his wife had died over a year earlier from cancer. He had four children, all older. All but one was married with small children. His older daughter, Faye, cooked dinner so we all could meet.

Figured they were just as interested in me. Sitting down for the fried chicken meal, I had discovered quickly enough that they knew everything about me. Kinda made me mad because I hadn't known about them.

He lived over in Marietta, which at first caused me some concern, but Mr. Lyndsey had said that we wouldn't be moving and understood how important it was for me to graduate at New Site. Guess he had accompanied Momma to some of our games last year. He said he was a big fan.

"Can't wait to see what you guys do this year."

Mr. Lyndsey had said the right things, but he just rubbed me the wrong way. His kids appeared happy for their dad and liked my mom. Everyone seemed just fine with the marriage except me.

Grandma told me not to cause any waves. Momma deserved to be happy.

I supposed she did.

The morning promised a sunny day. It was hot, but there was a nice breeze. There was just something about getting away from it all.

I heard a rustling in the bushes, followed by a quick movement through the tall grass. I saw a tail bob in the air. One of the bird dogs stopped and stood still. The other joined him standing motionless, one leg went up, and their tails pointed straight out.

Coach gestured for me to stay behind him and readied his gun on his shoulder. At Coach's whistle, the dogs flushed out the bird. A bobwhite quail took to the sky, but only for a moment. Coach fired, and the bird fell back down to earth.

"Go get it, Bill," Coach commanded, and the dog eagerly obeyed. In short order, Bill brought the dead bird back and dropped it into his master's hand. Coach patted his dog's head. "Good job."

Turning back to me, Coach handed me the bird.

"How many do you want today?"

"As many as we can get," I answered. "Momma wants to cook 'em for Mr. Lyndsey."

Coach nodded. "Good guy. Known the family for years. When is the big day?"

I frowned. "Labor Day weekend. Gives Mr. Lyndsey extra time off, being he works for the Post Office." I breathed out in a way I knew Coach would recognize as irritation. "You know what he told me...he said Momma told him how smart I am and said that when I graduate, he thinks he can get me on at the Post Office."

"Not exactly what you want to do, I take it." Coach gestured for us to keep walking.

"Nah, I mean I haven't decided exactly what I want to do," I said, keeping stride with him. "I'm not done with school yet."

"Not by a long shot." A broad smile crossed his face. "Senior year...It'll be the best one for you yet. It was for me."

I knew that Coach graduated from Marietta and had won their State title that year. Not surprisingly, Coach had been their best player. I had heard it said many times over that he could shoot the eyes off the basket.

"How was your senior year?"

"We won our State title, but only one year, not like you guys. But it was big around here. Don't think I could have done it without Coach Bullard. He taught me how to be a player." Coach stopped and lit up a cigarette. "I learned at an early age you can't let anyone dictate to you the person they think you are. It's up to you to become what you want to be.

"I never wanted to be like everyone else. Made my mother so mad when at eighth-grade graduation, I wore a brown suit instead of blue like everyone else. I wanted to stand out.

"Coach Bullard taught us how to win on an old dirt court. My dad didn't want me to play. Coach had to talk him into it. Dad needed me on the farm. I had to promise not to let basketball interfere with my chores. I had to do them when I got back home. Sometimes I didn't get done until ten at night, but I didn't complain because I got to play."

Coach took a puff and blew it out. "All my life, I never cared what others thought of me. Didn't listen to whispers behind my back; I just do what I believe is right. Doesn't mean it's not hard, and sometimes I failed at what I wanted to do, but I never…ever quit.

"After high school, I wanted to play on a Division I team. I was always told I was too slow and too short. No one would look at me or give me a chance. That's all I wanted was a chance. I played at Northeast, but afterward, I refused to give up. I never got to play for Kentucky but found a place on Mississippi State's team. Sometimes you have to make your chances."

There was something about the way Coach talked, that made you listen. It was like he knew what I was thinking and feeling.

"Funny thing. I ran into Coach Bullard the other day at the Hobo Station. We had a long talk. He wasn't down at the game but thought you guys put too much pressure on yourselves because you wanted to win it for me."

I rubbed my chin and shook my head. "I think about it a lot, Coach. I keep seeing that ball I let go to nowhere land. If…"

Coach chuckled. "If you had if I had…*if* is a big word. There isn't one of you boys that isn't blaming themselves for a missed opportunity. It is human nature. A ball lost at a crucial time; a man faked you out of your shoes to score or missing the last-second shot. It happens to us all. Like in life, there is never perfection.

"Reminds me of something Coach Bullard drilled into us boys, something I try and instill in you guys: pushing you always to give a hundred percent…because if you give everything, then you have nothing to hang your head about…No matter what happens, win or lose, you can accept it and move on."

Bill suddenly pointed, still as can be. Coach motioned to me that it was mine and then sent his dog to flush the bird. A moment later, the bird flew. I fired and shot it down.

"Not bad," Coach said. "You're getting better all the time."

"Yeah, I would love to hunt all summer, but I got a job with Mr. Sanders again, helping him out on his farm, but I will still help with your pepper field."

"Shouldn't be too much trouble." Coach took the bird from his birddog and looked back at me. "You know, we're not done."

No, I thought, feeling my competitive spirit rebound. We weren't done.

* * * *

"This year," Coach Carver began. "I don't think I have to coach you. You guys have been playing together for as long as I have been here. You know what to do and how to do it."

Coach put his coffee down on the bench and walked over to the blackboard. He wrote *Jackson!* and dotted it with emphasis.

"You are the most feared team in the state."

I sat by Larry, who was fixed on Coach's every word. From the corner of my eye, I saw my teammates. Coach was right. We did know each other well and depended on each other, knowing we would do our assignments.

There was a chip on my shoulder...our shoulders. Even after winning four consecutive state championships, we still had something to prove.

Over the summer, I had grasped that everyone was waiting for us to falter. I had run into Uncle Orson on the streets in Booneville while I had been out there with the guys playing pool. I hadn't seen him since Troy had passed.

Despite resenting my uncle for not seeing him for years, I couldn't help but like him. He had that personality that drew you to him.

"Good to see you, boy." Uncle Orson had patted my back. "You guys out at New Site have done good. Four in a row. Just can't seem to win the big one. Too bad. Cause this year, I feel its Thrasher's year."

I gave him a smile. Each year, everyone thought they could take us down, but I was sure my uncle was hoping. Ernie was a sophomore this year at Thrasher.

"Guess we'll see," I said, knowing Thrasher was a BB school. "Given that nobody in the county wants to play us, maybe it will be in Jackson."

"Yeah, that's because your coach is always up to one trick or another. He's just a snake in the grass."

Behind me, I heard my companions huff. Didn't blame the guys one bit. We took ribbing every time we went outside our community. We had heard it all. *Country bumpkins...so poor, don't have a pot to piss in, they're so dumb, they don't have the sense God gave a goose.*

But this was my uncle. He was family, you know. I wouldn't have even bothered to make a retort most of the time, but you don't talk about Coach like that. You just don't.

"Well, I reckon I understand why you would think that, Uncle Orson...being you can't perceive what it is like to win four State titles in a row. You're probably going to say that don't matter none: 'The past is in the past. It's this year.' Well, mark my word, we are going for five, and the overall title. You can take that to the bank."

I just kept on walking. Behind me, I laughed as Larry added, "We're going undefeated."

Larry wasn't one to brag, but I think it's what he believed. It was our mission this year. That, and taking the overall title.

There were five of us: Larry, Virgil, JC, Mickey, and me. There had been no words spoken, but we knew each other well enough to know that we wanted it in the worst way, and we had faith in each other that we would get it.

Listening to Coach, I comprehended that it was his vision. Nothing was going to be given to us. Winning the four titles meant that we knew how to win and what it took, but to win this year, we had to realize that teams weren't going to lay down for us. No one was going to give us anything.

We were going to face everyone's best game. To do that, we had to be at our best.

We would be.

Coach blew his whistle. Practice began.

* * * *

Sitting in the back of Coach Carver's class, I watched Coach walk into the room with a steaming coffee cup in hand. He was late, but I wasn't even supposed to be here.

I had just finished an English test in Mrs. Walker's class. She had sent me out so as not to disturb anyone else. I enjoyed Coach's class and sat quietly. He taught history: Mississippi and American.

Everyone was always on their best behavior in his class. If they weren't, they were given the choice between getting a paddling, or outlining a big old book. Coach told me once that he thought giving me a choice wouldn't work. He said that I would probably enjoy outlining the book.

No one would enjoy outlining a book, but I got his meaning. I liked to read.

Coach caught my eye and chuckled. This wasn't the first time I had done this, and I knew he didn't mind. Honestly, I enjoyed listening to him teach. He knew history and made it interesting. He loved to debate and would challenge your answer before telling whether it was right or not, as he was doing this morning to poor Ralph Cummings.

"You really believe that, Mr. Cummings?" Coach asked with that look that would make you question your own name.

Squirming in his seat, the skinny sophomore stuttered, "All I'm saying is that it's a free country. Why can't people demonstrate when they want to?"

Everyone had turned their attention on the kid. I knew what he felt. Mainly, he dearly wished he had never opened his mouth. At first, I had been that way before realizing that Coach wanted you to defend why you felt that way.

I couldn't help it. I raised my hand. "I'll take that, Coach."

"Well, Mr. Barnes, I would be extremely interested to hear your opinion."

Ralph breathed out a sigh of relief.

"Vietnam hasn't been a popular war. Many question why we are there," I said. "Given that we as American citizens have the right—the privilege—to express our opinion…."

Coach took in a deep breath. I realized I was about to bear the brunt of his argument. If there was one thing I knew about Coach Carver, it was that he was a patriot and an ex-Marine.

He rubbed his chin and then gestured toward me. "You believe it's your right to cause a ruckus, violently oppose authority, and burn the flag?"

I swallowed hard. I had asked for this. "I believe you are looking at the extremist. Most are peaceful…"

Taking a sip of his coffee, he looked at me. I knew it was coming.

"The rights you are asserting were given to us because of the bravery of soldiers just like the ones over in Vietnam. These long-haired draft dodgers are cowards," Coach said. "No man wants to go into a battle but remember our freedoms and those rights you talked about come with a price tag. Sacrifices have to be made by the citizens of a country such as America.

"Many young men are willing to make the ultimate sacrifice for their beliefs…to give you the freedom to protest. Because their country asked, they responded, understanding their responsibility. Tell me what their justification is? Because they don't like the war?"

Coach stood and moved to the front of his desk. He sat on it with one leg hanging over the corner. He went on, "Now, Mr. Barnes, you do have a valid point. We do have a right to question, but understand that with freedom comes responsibilities, which these draft dodgers are trying to wiggle out of by letting others do what they don't want to. It comes down to the fact that we are citizens of a country where there are laws to follow, whether we like it or not.

"Tell me, since you have already taken this class, what remedy do we have if we don't agree with how the country is run, or the state or county? What power do we hold?"

"The power of voting. Our vote counts," I answered without any hesitation.

"Remember, you can't complain if you don't vote. Don't forget that and use it."

The bell rang. Coach said one thing more before anyone could grab their books to move to the next class.

"I will say that if I were in charge, I wouldn't have gone into Vietnam without the expectation to win the damn war."

This time, I laughed to myself at the thought. Coach Carver probably would have won it in months instead of dragging it on for years.

* * * *

I stood in line behind Larry and waited to run onto the court. My last high school basketball season was about to begin, the start of a long road, and I was excited.

The season started on the road. We wouldn't have a home game until the end of November. Coach wasn't kidding about nobody in the county wanting to play us. We only had two county teams on the schedule this year, Booneville and Wheeler.

We would meet the other teams at some point. They couldn't run away from us forever. We did have the tournaments that we could hit them, and we did have Tupelo on the schedule this year.

My spirits were high when Larry dribbled out onto the court. I ran behind him with Coach's words echoing in me.

You believe this season starts tonight against Biggersville. It didn't. It started nine years ago…you were destined to play together…you are destined to win. This is our year.

Chapter Seventeen

Drenched in sweat, I fought for a position under the basket. Staring straight up, I saw the ball hit the rim. Immediately, I blocked my guy out and pushed back. Grappling for the rebound, I took it. One dribble out, and then I passed it to Larry, who pushed it up the court. Running down the court, I set in my corner. The ball returned to me, and I put it up. Swish.

The game clock wound down. With a quick glance over at Larry, I smiled. We had this one, a little closer than our other wins. We won by eight at the final buzzer even though it hadn't been as close as the score indicated.

We had annihilated our other opponents to this point. The previous week, we had beaten Winona by fifty.

In the locker room, Coach told us we had things to work on, but that it had been a good game. I was anxious to get going. I had told Linda I would drive her home if we won.

I wasn't in love or nothing, but I had started dating Linda over the summer. I liked her well enough, but I had warned her that ball came first during basketball season. She was a junior and understood or said she did.

She was a pretty girl with the most enormous brown eyes. I liked her laugh. Linda was friends with Roy's girlfriend. One day when I had gone over to his house, she had been there with Joan. After she told the funniest joke that her brother had told her, I asked her out.

We didn't do much but hang out at her house. I didn't have the money, but she didn't seem to mind. Besides, her father was kinda cool. He was a huge Royals fan.

"You could have passed it to me."

Looking up, I noticed J.C. still sitting in his uniform. It took me a moment to realize that he was talking to me. "What do you mean?"

"I was wide open under the basket, on your last shot. You had to have seen me. I was standing there with no one on me."

The bitterness riddled his voice.

"Sorry, man. I didn't. I'll catch you next time."

J.C. grimaced. "Yeah, right. No one passes to me…"

I let his words fade and didn't pay them much mind. Coach would have told me if I should have passed. Besides, Larry passed it to me, and I knew he wanted me to shoot.

Larry had an eye on the game. He had a knack for reading defenses. When I had first started playing for Coach, he would call out plays to Larry. Now, Coach had faith in his point guard, and only occasionally would Larry look over at Coach for help.

I reckoned I would call Larry a bulldog. Not only could he direct us on the court even if he was blindfolded, but he was also the best at dogging an opponent. I hated to admit that because I took pride in my defense, but Larry seemed to read his opponent like he read defenses.

When Coach asked who wanted to take the best player on the opposing team, Larry would volunteer with confidence that came from the belief that he could shut down anyone. His confidence was contagious. I don't think any of us believed that we couldn't carry out an assignment.

I grabbed my bag and headed out the door. Linda was waiting for me.

* * * *

Dadgummit! J.C. had thrown up another brick. We had a hard enough time getting a good shot to give it up on a contested one. Not to mention, Virgil had been open on the wing.

The semi-finals at the Baldwyn tournament weren't going as planned. We trailed Wheeler by three with less than a minute to go. Mickey grabbed the rebound and laid it up for two.

We jumped on them as soon as they took the ball out. Wheeler lunged it down court. J.C. picked it off. I took a quick glance over at Coach. He signaled a time-out, but J.C. must not have seen him. He drove toward the basket. The problem with that was, he was mid-court. Wheeler's quick guard stole it. A second later, Wheeler's guard stole it and threw it to one of their forwards, who laid it in for two right before the buzzer.

Dang, it all! We lost.

I didn't have to look at Coach to know he wasn't happy, but there again, neither were we. We had lost our bid for an undefeated season.

Bright and early the next morning, I sat on the bleachers with the other guys as Coach paced in front of us. He hadn't started talking, but we all knew what was coming. We had lost a game we shouldn't have.

Coach turned to us. He pressed his lips together tightly like he was thinking hard. "This morning, I think you guys should tell me what happened last night."

He pointed at Larry. "You start."

Larry looked at J.C. "He shot too much. If you aren't hitting, stop shooting."

"I was open," J.C. said defensively. "Whatever happened to *win as a team and lose as a team.*"

"This isn't about pointing blame," Coach said. "I think you guys have some growing frustrations that need to be expelled."

"It certainly feels like everyone is ganging up on me," J.C. retorted.

Beside me, I heard Virgil huff. Myself, I couldn't contain my irritation. "Come on, J.C., you ignored Coach when he tried to call a time-out. I saw you. Instead, you lost the ball."

J.C. stared at me for a long moment, stood, and walked out.

* * * *

I couldn't believe it. J.C. had quit.

Stunned, but also mad, we continued. In the next two games, we won handily by twenty-one and forty-four, respectively. Yet, it didn't feel right. I didn't feel right.

About a week after J.C. walked out on us, Coach talked to me after practice. "Have you seen J.C.?"

I shook my head. "Don't reckon I will neither. I think I'm the last person he wants to see."

"You think so?" Coach asked. "Heard he hasn't been to school for the last three days. Thought you two were close."

Shrugging, I said, "No more than the rest of us."

After dinner, I sat down to watch TV with Grandma, but I couldn't get Coach's words out of my head. I got up.

"Grandma, I'm going out, and I'll be back soon."

"Not to Linda's, I hope, at this hour."

Shaking my head, I answered, "No, to a friend's."

"J.C.'s?"

I nodded.

Coach had been right. J.C. was a friend. I had known him forever.

Grandma knew J.C. had quit the team. I had told her everything since it was only the two of us now.

Momma and Mr. Lyndsey officially lived with us but they stayed most nights over at his house. Momma said they didn't want to cause me any problems with basketball. I appreciated that, and, to be honest, it was more comfortable this way.

Mr. Lyndsey was nice, but I didn't know him. He tried, though.

He brought Momma to every game. I had even seen his kids in the stands, cheering for me. He had even promised to help bring Grandma to the County Tournament. It was at Northeast, and it would be easier for her to attend in her wheelchair.

Pulling into J.C.'s driveway, I saw him sitting on his front porch with his hound dog. He wouldn't look at me. Instead, he lowered his gaze and frowned.

My immediate hope was that he wouldn't go back into the house. Thankfully, he didn't.

I stopped at the steps. Placing my foot on the bottom one, I leaned forward. "Came to check on you."

"Well, now, you've seen me, you can go."

"I…," I suddenly became lost for words. "Man, I want you to come back."

"Why?" He looked up at me. "You don't need me."

Looking at him, I noticed a bottle of beer sitting next to his foot. It was open but still full. "I need you…we all do."

"Not by the scores," he sniffled. "Sally told me that you guys demolished Belden…right before she broke up with me."

"Sorry, man…women!" I exclaimed, trying hard to empathize with him. "Fickle."

J.C. huffed. "Yeah, she kept at me about scoring more. Wanted my name in the paper like you guys…wanted to brag about it, I guess. Wasn't worth bragging about dating a nameless man."

"How can you say that? Where would we be without your rebounds, and how you match up with the big guys? Don't know where you get an idea like that. You're in the paper more than me. Honestly, the only one that's there all the time is Virgil. Suppose if anyone has a right to complain, it's Larry. He gives the ball up to us all the time.

Besides, with you gone, Coach is rotating me inside. Don't like it.”

“Not how Linda sees it,” J.C. looked straight at me. “She told Sally that you would get more shots if I would throw it to you in the corner. Said you were irritated with me.”

“Nah, Linda wouldn't have said anything like that, 'cause I never said that. I do my job, just like you. I mean, man, I've known you forever. Lordy be! If you had a problem with me, why didn't you come to me?”

“I tried. You brushed me off.”

Thinking back, I remembered once…maybe I should have paid more attention. My mind had been elsewhere.

“I'm not brushing you off now,” I said. “Starting this season, I had a lot of dreams, but they included all of us. It won't be the same if you're not there.”

“Reckon it's not up to me.”

Shaking my head, I asked, “Why not?”

“Coach said it would be up to you guys. He said I let you guys down.”

I stared at J.C. as comprehension swept through me. Coach had set me up. He had already talked to J.C..; of course he had.

“Well, you know what my answer is.”

“It's hard to come back and face the guys…Our bid for an undefeated season was lost.”

“All it means is that we take the title,” I shrugged. “Nothing less than the title, but for now, what if I walk in with you? Would that help?”

“Might,” he said, bending over and pouring out the beer. “It's warm, anyway.”

The next day, we voted to let J.C. come back. He was waiting outside sitting against a car's hood when I went to get him. We walked back inside together, and J.C. apologized to all of us.

Coach said, "That's that." He blew his whistle, and we jumped out on the court to get practice underway.

It felt right. Better than right. Sometimes we might get mad at each other, but once said, it was done and over.

There again, we had a mission.

My mission would be without a girlfriend. I broke up with Linda. I didn't know if she had really said anything or not. I didn't ask. It was just this season was more important to me.

The funny thing was, J.C. made up with Sally, but for me, I didn't want another distraction.

Chapter Eighteen

Each year, the County Tournament was played at Northeast. The junior college gym was larger than any other of the teams participating. Walking into the gym, you crossed over a small practice court. On the far end, there was another one where they would pull out the portable bleachers when needed. For this tournament, those bleachers would be needed.

The main court was in the middle. I wasn't particularly fond of playing on it. Mainly, I didn't like the baskets being opened. I was used to walls defining my view. It never failed, it would take me a couple of shots in a game to get into my groove.

The previous year, I had made a complete fool out of myself by stealing the ball, not once or twice, but three times and missing the ensuing lay-up. The guys hadn't let me forget it either, especially since, on the last miss, I had let out a word that everyone could hear.

This year, the Banner Independent promoted the tournament as the best teams in the state going after each other. Our first game was against Booneville. Thankfully, I didn't do anything embarrassing and had a decent game.

Later that night, Thrasher was playing Baldwyn before our game against Wheeler in the semi-finals.

The gym was packed, and I was excited. Grandma was sitting courtside under the goal in a wheelchair. It had become easier for her to move in it instead of using her crutches. Momma and Mr. Lyndsey had come early and gotten her the spot in between the lines of folding chairs.

Surprisingly, I noticed Uncle Orson had moved into Mr. Lyndsey's chair. Knowing my uncle, he had come late for the Thrasher game and had talked his way into a front-row seat. It irked me, but Grandma was laughing.

I stared at her for a time. She looked so happy. I knew I was. She hadn't gotten to see me play much. I could hear the stories she would be telling me about Uncle Orson because I knew Grandma didn't care for Uncle Orson. She was up to something.

Larry punched my shoulder. It was time to go get dressed. We had a game to play.

Focus was the name of the game. Wheeler wasn't about to lay down and let us have our revenge win. You might beat us once, but not twice.

Yet, the game was nip and tuck. The lead was going back and forth all night. We couldn't seem to break away from them. With the game winding down, we were losing by one, and they had the ball.

From the corner, Wheeler's forward shot and missed. Mickey pulled down the rebound. I took off down the sidelines with only twelve seconds to go. Mickey hit me.

Dribbling up on the wing, I glanced at my Grandma. I had never taken the winning shot before; this could be the time. From the corner of my eye, I saw a defender gaining on me, but J.C. was under the basket.

In my head, I heard the clock count down. Instinct took over. I passed it to J.C., who laid it in for the win.

Only afterward, I felt a tinge of regret for not shooting the last shot, but the moment passed. We had won the game; that was the most important fact.

Coach gave me a nod. He understood you give it to the open guy with the high percentage shot. The win is about the team.

We won to play in the finals the next night against Baldwyn. I was a little disappointed. I wanted Thrasher. I wanted to play the team that had refused to play us during the regular season. Now, it seemed the only way to meet them would be in the Grand Slam.

Sometime during the first half, Uncle Orson and his family had left. I had caught a glimpse of Mr. Lyndsey sitting by Grandma. I was sure my uncle had snuck out.

Grandma got home before me but was waiting up to talk. She was anxious to tell me about her night.

"You did right at the end of the game," she started. "I hope Coach told you."

Laughing to myself, Coach would have told me if I hadn't made the pass, but instead, I said, "He made a point of it in the locker room."

She smiled real big. "You played so well. You done real good. You've got such a nice shot, and you scored so many points…fifteen."

I grinned. She had counted every one of them. I was glad she had gotten to come.

Grandma talked to me about Uncle Orson. She told me that he had been quite informative. He had gone on and on about how good Thrasher was this year. How they were going all the way. They weren't going to settle just for the State title. No way; the overall title was what they had their sights on, and according to my uncle, he had no doubt. New Site's days were over.

"I let him talk for a bit," Grandma said. "Then, after Thrasher lost, I told him outright, this is New Site's glory year. I said I knew for a fact because my grandson is on the Royals, a kid that he'd turned his back on, but that you've turned out just fine."

"I love you."

I hugged her tight. I had a sudden realization that she needed that moment. For years, she must had felt helpless. So much of her life hadn't been in her control. Her husband had died of a heart attack leaving her on her own. She developed diabetes and lost a leg. She had watched her youngest daughter marry an alcoholic bum. She took two fatherless boys under her wing and had her heart ripped out when one died. She was tired of being looked down at by the likes of Orson Barnes. She didn't have much…we didn't have much, but we had each other.

I vowed I would make her proud.

The next night, Grandma came for the finals and sat in the same place. I focused on the game, and the open goals didn't seem to affect me as they had before. I think I only missed one shot and stole the ball a couple of times. We beat Baldwyn by eleven.

The Royals were crowned best in the county— once again.

* * * *

The playoffs were about to begin. I sat in the locker room and waited to play Marietta, our first opponent in District.

We had ended the regular season with a 25-2 record. We had lost one other game when we went against Baldwyn in a regular-season game. Overall, I felt pretty confident about our chances.

This was what I had been waiting for all season—the road to the championship.

Marietta hadn't had a good year. As a matter of fact, they were pretty bad, going by their record. Coach warned us not to judge them by how many games they had won or lost. A new season began tonight. Our records meant nothing.

The Royals were bidding for our fifth straight title.

"Thinking you're good will get you beat," Coach said. "Get your head straight to play. You can't just turn it on and off."

Coach took a puff on his cigarette. Throwing it on the ground, he extinguished it with his shoe and exhaled. "It's time, boys. Remember, one game at a time."

Inside the packed Belmont gym, the District games began. I looked up and saw Missy beside Momma. I wondered if they would get to go to Jackson this year.

Warm-ups didn't go well with me. For some reason, I couldn't get the feel of the ball. I always liked to end on a make. It gave me an extra bit of confidence. Tonight, though, I couldn't get it in as the buzzer blew.

As I made my way into the huddle before tip-off, Coach shook his head. "You guys better get it together, or we'll be going home tonight."

Nodding, I said, "We've got this, Coach."

But we didn't. Immediately it was apparent that Marietta hadn't gotten the news that we were the better team. Don't think they cared. They were all over us.

Virgil shot from the corner and missed. J.C. got the rebound but missed the easy put-back. Simple executions were botched. Balls were thrown away.

Marietta had come to play. We hadn't.

I attempted a steal. Instead, my guy got past me for an easy two. Coach called a time-out.

"You do realize we are playing for our lives," he said, pointing to the court. "Not one of you is hitting your assignments. You're a step behind. Pick it up!"

Running back on the court, I had every intention of doing just that. It was just that my feet and hands wouldn't do what I wanted. I couldn't buy a bucket. Try as I might on defense, I was tripping over myself.

One of their guys, Lonnie Johnston, couldn't miss. I knew of him. He lived down the road from Mr. Lyndsey. He was everywhere on the court.

We were losing at the half. As was to be expected, Coach was mad.

His message was heard loud and clear. "There isn't anything I can do for you boys. This isn't about a play that will break it open. It isn't about getting someone a shot. It's about heart. That comes from you. You have to dig in and don't let go."

The third quarter saw Marietta come out with fire in their blood. The realization swept through me that this was going to be a dog fight. Marietta wasn't going to roll over.

Throwing the ball in to Larry, he dribbled up to my side. He said, "Fight."

Larry called out Mickey's play. I ran to the right side and picked for J.C. Cutting through, J.C. took the ball and shot. Missed. I rebounded and put it up...missed again, but I fought through the block out and finally laid it in.

Mickey stole the inbound pass. With a light touch, he bounced it to Virgil, who hit his shot. For the first time in the game, we were leading. It wasn't over yet.

Johnston up faked me almost out on my shoes. I reached out and fouled him. It was my fourth, and I had only been guarding him since the half. He had already made twelve free throws. This time though, he missed both.

Back and forth over the court, we hung onto the lead. With the seconds ticking away, Johnston went around me again. J.C. came up and fouled him. I watched Lonnie walk up to the line knowing these free throws wouldn't make a difference. We had stretched our lead to four. Lonnie missed again. I came down with the rebound and threw it over to Larry, who dribbled it until the final buzzer.

There wasn't the usual jubilant celebration after the win. It was more relief. I was exhausted. Leaning over, I grasped my legs to catch my breath. I looked up and caught the expression on Johnston's face.

Honestly, it was the first time I had thought about how my opponent felt. I saw the bitter disappointment and realized that it could have been me.

In silence, I walked back to the locker room beside Larry. We didn't even change our shoes as we waited on Coach. It seemed an eternity before he stepped inside.

For a long moment, Coach stared at us. Then, he breathed out.

"Each and every one of you should get down on your knees and thank the good Lord, for it was only by his grace that we won. Boys, we got out-played. Marietta came to win, plain and simple. We didn't...and we should have known better.

"I told you that you can't get it going if you didn't come to play. You can't just turn it on and off." He pressed his lips tightly together, seemingly suppressing his anger at our performance. "Marietta played like I want you guys to play, like it could be your last game. They left everything on the court but take the game for what it was. Sometimes we get lucky, and this was one of those times. We have tomorrow."

I nodded in agreement and stood to get dressed. I had only untied my sneakers when Coach gestured for one more thing. Rubbing his chin, he grimaced.

"You guys need to realize that if you play another game like this, we won't be going anywhere."

He turned and walked out.

* * * *

Restless, I needed to get out of the house. Grandma had long gone to sleep. I should have gone to bed, too. It had been a long weekend, and I had school in the morning.

Instead, I got the keys to the car. Walking outside, I heard the crickets chirping in the distance. For a time, I stared at the vastness of the night sky filled with sparkling stars. I was struck by the peacefulness of the night.

I felt a sudden sadness. I missed my brother. I needed Troy, and he wasn't here. *But did he know?*

Getting into the car, I knew where I was going. Didn't really know why. I didn't have keys to get into the gym and

certainly couldn't ask for them at this time of night.
Everyone would be in bed by now. It was past eleven.

Yet, when I pulled into the parking lot, I saw Coach's
blue Chevy truck, which didn't shock me. After our
weekend, I was sure that Coach wouldn't be sleeping for a
while, knowing him.

Walking onto the eerily quiet court, I called out to
Coach. A moment later, he walked out of his office with a
broad smile.

"Dean, what are you doing here? You should be
getting your sleep. It's going to be a long week."

Nodding, I agreed. "I tried."

He gave me one of those looks that told me that he
understood. He turned and left me for a minute, coming
back with a ball in his hands. He threw it to me.

In the middle of the dimly lit court, I dribbled down
and took a jump shot. Swish! Suddenly, the gym was lit.
Coach had gone to turn on the lights.

"Sometimes, you just need to work it out," Coach said.
"Shoot around all you want."

"Coach…" I rebounded my shot. "Thanks. I needed to
say that."

"Not a problem," Coach said. "I can't sleep either.
There are a million things I have to get done."

"I know. It's strange, isn't it?" I shot again. "I've
wanted to play Thrasher all year, and it's in the semi-finals
of the Grand Slam. My cousin is on the team."

Coach nodded. "I know the kid. Ernie Barnes, a
sophomore. Not much playing time yet."

I smiled with the comprehension that Coach probably
already knew the players on Thrasher better than their own
coach. I figured that was why he was here tonight, studying
his scouting notes on the team we would face on Friday in
Jackson. Probably easier here than at home with his four
little kids.

After the Marietta scare, we had demolished every team we faced. Most of our wins were by twenty to twenty-five points. We had faced our county rival Jumpertown three times, each time in the finals. We destroyed them in the District and North Half finals.

Jumpertown had eliminated Wheeler in District. The Cardinals were one of the county teams we hadn't faced until the playoffs. Like Thrasher, they had refused to schedule any regular-season games with us. Yet, we had gotten to see them enough over the last few weeks.

Other teams got to move on through the playoffs by coming in second or third place. We had always won our way through. During my time on the Royals, we hadn't lost a playoff game in the Class B State tournament. Troy's team hadn't lost either. It was quite a winning streak.

Coach laid out our assignments, and we carried them out. If we needed an adjustment, Coach had it. We trusted he would have an answer. He had never failed us.

In turn, we hadn't failed him. We played like the team we were. No one was above another. We had played together since grammar school. We knew each other well.

The Tupelo Journal had called attention to the great ball being played in hill country. They called Northeast Mississippi the state's basketball hotbed. Three teams from Prentiss County had won their State title: Baldwyn, Thrasher, and New Site.

The Royals had won five consecutive titles. The paper said that no other ball club had dominated the scene so completely.

This year in the State finals against Jumpertown for the third time, we had faced a hard battle. We were losing at half by seven. Coach would have none of it.

I'll never forget Coach walking in with his red towel over his shoulder. He had that determined look like we were about to take down our adversary.

"We're not going to be in here long. We have a game to win and can't do it from here."

He outlined a full-court press and a simple change to our offense.

"You have played hard and deserved everything that has come your way. We have two more quarters to go. Do not accept anything but a victory. Believe in yourselves, and in your teammates. Together, boys, we're going to take this game. It's ours. Now get out there and play ball!"

We exploded in the third. The game and the State title were ours.

Returning this afternoon, we had been given a hero's welcome once again in Booneville—a victory caravan. I had been beyond exhausted but still couldn't get to sleep. It's why I came to the gym tonight. I needed to shoot around.

I bounced the ball a couple of times and then held it. "Coach," I said before he turned back to his office. "You know I have dreamed of this since I was a little kid watching Troy..."

"He would be so proud of the player you've become, Dean. You know that, don't you?"

"Yeah." I breathed out, and to my horror, tears welled in my eyes. "It's just...that this is my last chance, Coach. I've watched others leave without taking the over-all championship...I want to do this...for Troy...for you...for the Royals...but I got this pit in the bottom of my stomach like I'm scared to play..."

He shook his head. "No one on my team ever walks away a loser even if we didn't win State, which I'll remind you is quite the accomplishment. Nothing to hang your head about. But don't be afraid to win. Just do your best. That's all you can do."

For a brief moment, he looked down at the floor, then back up at me. "Son, life isn't easy. You know how hard it can be, but this is a good moment. Savor it."

Coach reached out his hands for the ball. I passed it to him and watched him take a shot from point and sink it.

He turned back to me. "Dean, you're a smart kid. You're going to be fine, but you know where I'm at if you need me."

I knew that, but it was good to hear.

Coach went back into his office. I went back to shooting. For the next hour, I shot free-throws.

When I left, Coach was still in his office.

Chapter Nineteen

"He's yours," Larry called on the pick.

Immediately, I was on him like a bee on honey. I wasn't gonna let go, either. Larry was dogging Thrasher's leading scorer and wouldn't let go of him. Pestering the dickens out of him, Jackie Smith couldn't find the bucket. Thrasher's coach was trying to figure out a way to free him up.

It wasn't gonna happen. Not today.

We may not have played Thrasher before, but we knew them well by the time we hit the court. Coach Carver had an answer for everything they were throwing at us.

"Thrasher normally plays a two-one-two defense and is a run-and-gun team. Several times this year, they have scored over a hundred points," Coach said. Drawing on his blackboard, he showed us what we were going to do to shut them down. "This is the team that didn't want to play us. Let's show they can't run from us now."

From the start of the game, Thrasher's coach tried to outmaneuver Coach Carver. They hit us with a one-three-one defense, which set Virgil and me up in our corners. We were having a field day.

The game started with Mickey taking the ball and driving in for a lay-up. Taking the ball back up court, I could tell that their point guard was looking to pass it. Larry stepped into the passing lane keeping the ball from Smith. In desperation, the guard heaved the ball from half-court toward the goal…and hit it.

Lucky shot, but it was the only lucky thing that was happening to them.

With the game tied at five, Virgil and I hit five unanswered baskets. The high scoring Thrasher was unable to get into a rhythm. We all stuck like glue to our men.

From the corner, I put in another two. Looking up in the stands, I allowed myself to smile. Missy was sitting with Grandma. Jackson coliseum had a place for people in wheelchairs to watch the game.

Missy had taken off from work at Booneville Hospital, where she now worked. It was hard because so many others wanted the time off, but somehow or other, Missy had put in for it before our season had even started.

"Not going to miss this one," she told me. "Troy would want me there."

On top of that, she had brought Grandma with her, not allowing Grandma to spend a dime.

"I already have a hotel room. It would have been a waste of a bed if I didn't bring someone with me."

I had never seen Grandma so happy. She had said she had a little saved and was going to pay for their food, but I knew Missy wasn't going to allow it.

Momma and Mr. Lyndsey were down too. A couple of his kids had come along. This was big for Prentiss County, to have three teams in the finals. No one wanted to miss it.

I knew that my dad's family was there too but I hadn't heard a word from any of them. I was sure they were up in the stands somewhere. Somehow it didn't matter to me today.

The people that cared about me were there.

I saw my cousin at warm-ups. We talked for a second and wished each other luck. I had nothing against him—liked him, really—but I wanted to beat Thrasher bad. I realized that he probably wouldn't even set foot on the court unless it was a blow-out.

It was—ours.

With a few minutes left in the game, Coach began to put the subs into the game. Watching from the bench, I saw the clock count down.

There was no suspense. We won eighty-one to fifty-six.

This was it. Unbelievably, we were going back to the finals.

I was ecstatic, and for the first time I was able to share my joy with my family. After hugging my teammates and getting a handshake from Coach, I went in search of them.

This had been the best game I had ever played. I scored seventeen points, stole balls, and picked off passes. Virgil had scored over thirty, but that was Virgil. That's what he did. Larry had kept their leading scorer in the single digits when his average had been over twenty-five a game.

Mickey…J.C.…We all played well. The win felt good.

Making my way through the crowd, a man turned into me—Uncle Orson. His expression betrayed his reluctance to see me, but he extended his hand.

"Good game."

"Thanks." I accepted. It was easy to be gracious when we had just beaten them.

Uncle Orson grimaced and started to walk around me.

I don't know what possessed me, instead of just letting him walk away, I said, "While you're here, why don't y'all stay a day and see us bring home the trophy."

Surprisingly, he nodded. "We might just do that, Dean…good luck."

* * * *

My focus had been on Thrasher. I hadn't thought about the next game until we had beaten them.

Tonight, this would be my last high school basketball game.

I suddenly didn't want the season to end, and in the same breath, I wanted us to play as soon as we could. We had gone back and watched Baldwyn and Wingfield play. Wingfield came from behind and beat Baldwyn by seven.

We faced a towering problem.

According to the papers the next morning, no one gave us a legitimate shot at the title. Logically, it made sense if you just looked at the stats. I mean, we were one of the smallest schools in the state facing the largest. Their freshman class was larger than our entire school.

We were from a small farming community. They were situated in Jackson, the largest city in Mississippi.

I didn't care. Coach said they could only put five players on the court at one time just like us…except their five were huge, and they had the two most-recruited players in the state. One was six-six and the other six-seven.

Mickey frowned when he glanced over the article. "They gave Wingfield three-fourths a page, and here we are at the end of it. Barely a mention. They do realize that this is our fifth consecutive title, right? And third consecutive finals."

"We don't pay them much mind," Larry said. "Let them think that. We are going to take down those arrogant sons of…"

"Ouch, Larry," I cut him off. We were sitting in the middle of IHOP. "We get the point."

"Yeah, but the papers have guaranteed a Wingfield victory…their coach said it at least three times in this article." Larry laid down his paper. "Their coach is quoted as saying they weren't worried about Baldwyn, but Baldwyn almost had them."

I had heard Coach Carver say that Wingfield had two great players on their team. It was the best team he had seen this year with very few weaknesses, but he had also said we were going to take them down.

Wingfield wasn't a humble team by a long shot. They had only lost four games this year. When they won, they celebrated in their opponents' faces. They tried to downgrade and humiliate the teams.

So much so, that after the semi-final game, one of the Baldwyn boys came up to us.

"Take 'em down. Beat their butts."

We were going to give it our best shot.

It was going to be a long day waiting for tonight.

* * * *

Sitting in the locker room, I waited until it was time to line up. My heart raced in anticipation of the game.

Outside these walls, it seemed all of Prentiss County had come to cheer us on to victory. The heart of basketball country wanted this title against this condescending team, who thought all they had to do was show up to win.

Granted, even all of Prentiss County couldn't compare to the crowd from Wingfield. They had the entire city of Jackson rooting for them to win.

Who could ever consider us country boys contenders for the crown? J.C. said we were going to show them how country boys play.

I wasn't thinking about the past. Tonight, I was thinking about what was in front of me.

Pride of being a Royal surged through me.

Missy, Grandma, and Momma sat anxious for me, but tonight I would be okay. Coach said to do our best—it was all anyone could do. I was prepared to do just that.

Other players had come by to wish us luck: Rich, Freddie, Jimmy, Donnie, and I swear it must have been the entire Royal family. Donnie gave me a look and a pat on the back. He didn't say anything, but I knew he was thinking of Troy.

Troy was never far from my mind and heart. I knew my brother was here with me.

Coach came into the locker room, carrying a confident air about him. He regarded us for a long moment and smiled.

"You boys are ready. You have been working for this chance all year. We have been here before and know what it takes to do the impossible. I had a reporter ask me yesterday did I really think we have a chance. I told him we have never taken the court without the expectation to win.

"I know, I know; I hear it too. No one else believes we can do this. Do not accept anything except victory. This is ours." He pointed toward the door. "Out there is the largest crowd in the history of high school ball waiting to watch this game. Make no mistake: most are here to see us lose.

"No one—no one—thinks we are going to win, except us."

Coach took a deep breath. "I have never cared about what other people think. They don't know us. They don't have faith in our ability. They don't see our heart and determination. But make no mistake: by the end of this game, they will."

The air was thick with anticipation when we ran onto the court.

I heard someone yell out, "You've got to be kidding me. They look like a grammar school team. Ain't no way they will beat Wingfield."

I paid it no mind. I was thinking of what Coach had told us.

They like to fast break. We have to stop it. When we shoot free-throws, we need two people back on defense. Jump on them as soon as they rebound. Keep the pressure on them. We are going to press— a one-two-two. We aren't going to let them get started.

Number 50 has a temper. Stay on him; dog him. It will frustrate him and take him out of his game. Number 15 and 20 snowbird. Keep your head up. Make them play our game.

When the buzzer sounded ending warm-ups, it felt like my heart was in my throat. I caught a glance of Wingfield's two big men, Sutton and Johnson. They were laughing and sharing a joke with their point guard, Chase.

This was it. Funny thing: an eerie calm swept through me when the official threw the ball up for the opening tip-off.

I heard a voice say *Just play your game. Just play.*

Height won first possession, but immediately I pounced on their guard. He turned it over to Larry, who grabbed it and tossed it over to Virgil, who sank two from the right wing. *Always a good sign when Virgil hit his first one.*

The thought was fleeting. As soon as we scored, we hit them with our press. Wingfield couldn't get the ball over half-court. Their guy, Smart, pushed me when Mickey and I had him trapped in the corner.

The official called a foul. The Wingfield forward threw his hands up in frustration. He turned around to his bench. "Coach, something has to be done. Something bad illegal is going on out here. They must have six players on the court!"

We had definitely got under their skin, but Wingfield wasn't giving up. It was early. They took the lead with seven minutes to go in the first quarter, but Larry hit Virgil in the corner for another two on our next possession.

Frustrating the Falcons, we gave them fits with the press. Larry would call whether we hit them with a full-court or dropped back to a half. They absolutely didn't like it when we blocked out. Time and time again, they were called for fouls going over our backs.

Taking the brunt of Wingfield's frustration, Larry was constantly on the free-throw line. Wasn't a good move on their part. Larry was a ninety-two percent free-throw shooter.

Virgil nailed one shot after another. I hadn't had many opportunities to shoot. I was in a battle underneath the basket with one of their big men. J.C. had the other.

The second quarter was dwindling down with only seconds left. Larry dribbled the ball down over mid-court. I thought Larry was going to shoot it. Instead, he threw it over to me on the left wing. I hadn't a choice but to launch it before the buzzer went off. Unbelievably, it went in.

At the half, we had a ten-point lead.

Whatever Coach said to us in the locker room, I only half remembered. I just heard him telling me, "You're doing good."

I realized one thing. I was in a battle. Those guys were big and rough, but I wasn't backing down, determined to get as many rebounds as I could off misses.

The third began as the second had ended. It didn't seem that their coach had made any adjustments because they kept fouling Larry, who hadn't missed. But it really didn't matter who they fouled. Everyone hit their free throws, except me. I hadn't been fouled.

We hadn't gone without fouling, though. Virgil, J.C., and I were in foul trouble with three fouls each, but it didn't stop our aggressive defense.

Our lead had built to twelve early in the fourth when the ref called a foul on Sutton. Their coach blew his lid. He stomped out onto the court with steam coming from his ears.

"You just want to give them the game! They're the ones that are pressing…and you're calling fouls on us! What a raw deal!"

Immediately, the official's hand signaled a T. "Technical."

"I shouldn't expect any more from you than that," Wingfield's coach huffed. "I have never seen worse officiating."

From the other side of the court, the other official made his way over to the Wingfield coach. "Take a seat, Coach, or I'll eject you. Officiating has nothing to do with the score. You're getting your butt outplayed and outcoached. Get back to your bench or leave."

For a minute, I thought the coach was going to snap. His face had gone beet red, but he turned on his heels and made his way back to his seat.

The game slowed down. I was tired, realizing I had been playing on adrenaline. We had increased the lead to fourteen with just over five minutes left to play. Then Virgil got called for his fourth foul.

Coach called a time-out with one clear message. "Whatever you do, Virgil, don't foul."

The next time down the court, Virgil fouled. He was done. A few seconds after, so was J.C. Roy came into the game, and then Billy. Wingfield lost their two big men shortly after, but momentum had changed.

With four and a half minutes on the game clock, Wingfield went on the offensive. They pressed. Larry tried to get the ball to Mickey but got picked off. The next time down, Travis threw it away.

They were all over us. We were holding on for dear life. I looked up at the clock. Our lead had vanished. We were only leading by two. Roy had the ball but was cornered on the sidelines by two defenders. The whistle blew. Traveling.

I glanced over at the bench. Coach Carver sat with the twisted red towel in hand. He gestured with his hand for calm. I heard him say, "Just play ball."

Nodding, I ran to pick up my guy down under the basket and stuck like glue. Larry was on the point guard at mid-court, who threw over to the wing. The guy shot one-handed. It was airborne but wasn't even close.

Immediately, I turned and blocked out my guy. I brought down the errant ball. Almost instantly, I was fouled.

Looking up at the scoreboard, I saw there were only sixteen seconds left. We had a two-point lead.

Larry came up and slapped my shoulder. "You've got this."

But it wouldn't be until after a time-out. Then another one. Wingfield tried to freeze me out by calling, not one, but two, time-outs.

Coach didn't say a word to me. He told Larry, Roy and Travis to stay back on defense. Don't foul, and not to give them a shot if I hit my free-throws. If I missed, to play hard defense, and not let them get a shot off.

I was left to my thoughts. I didn't have to be told that if I hit my free throws, victory would be sealed. If I didn't…well, I didn't want to think of what could happen.

Instead, I thought of Troy…when he told me he was joining the Air Force. *I will be bragging about you being on the best basketball team in the state. The things you're going to achieve. I see it now.*

Walking up to the line, I saw nothing but the goal in front of me, like I had done a million times. I could hear Coach tell me *Gotta get those free throws down, Dean. Can't win if you don't hit those.*

Bouncing the ball once, I set to shoot. One deep breath, and I released the ball. For an eternity, it sailed.

…and the fans went wild.

Epilogue

No matter how much time has passed, I will never forget the sound of the crowd exploding. The coliseum shook. Never had I expected that most there would have been rooting for us by night's end.

Basketball glory! We had won the overall title, seventy-four to seventy-two. Wingfield drove down in the final seconds and scored an easy basket to draw to within two points. Without giving them a chance to set a defense, I threw the ball in to Larry, who held it until the buzzer sounded.

Wingfield had no time-outs to call. They had used them all against me to freeze me out. I believed they had thought I would collapse under the pressure.

Coach said they didn't know my heart. He told me that there are some moments one is born for; this one was mine.

Who would have ever imagined a bunch of scrawny country boys would have won the Grand Slam?

Returning home, we met a hero's welcome. Over a hundred cars paraded into Booneville from Frankstown. Booneville's high school band played; speeches were made.

Prentiss County was proud of our accomplishment. We had brought home the Grand Slam title.

Looking back now, I wondered if Coach Carver realized what he had truly done. It wasn't only winning the championship. He had defined our community as winners.

I left after graduation and did what Troy had planned. I joined the Air Force. After four years, I went to college and got my degree in journalism.

Dispensing with modesty, I realize my career has been distinguished, serving as a Middle East correspondent for over twenty years. I earned a reputation for my fearlessness in reporting and the ability to gain access to notoriously inaccessible figures. After returning, I wrote a syndicated column and published eight books.

My phone vibrates. It's Jack looking for me again. Soon, he will talk to his sister, and then, Kelly will be calling. Debby, my wife of thirty-five years, must have told our children I hadn't returned from the hospital.

I have come home to see Missy, my dear friend—more than a friend, a sister—who was in the hospital with congestive heart failure. She was the last of my family down here. At least, the family I had kept in touch with over the years. Grandma passed away less than a year after I graduated from complications with diabetes. Momma died peacefully in her sleep around ten years back, right after Mr. Lyndsey.

God love Missy. She was what they called good people around here. She was loyal to Troy's memory for thirteen years before she married a local guy from Booneville and had three children.

Early this morning, Debby and I flew into Tupelo. I dropped Debby off at the hotel. She realized I needed to see Missy alone for a time.

Granted, the drive from the hospital to our hotel room was only five minutes, but when I got back in the rental car after Missy went to sleep, I drove to New Site by myself. Feeling nostalgic, I suppose. It was contrary to my normal behavior.

There comes a time when the ghosts of the past consume us when the past and present collide. Mine had come today with my return to the place of my birth.

Whether good or bad, our youth decides the character of the man we become. It was no different for me.

Even though I haven't lived here for decades, this was home, where I was born and raised. I left, but it never left me.

Despite my melancholy mood, I didn't want to worry Debby. I took a moment and texted her I would be back soon. She didn't need to worry. I was fine...just remembering my youth.

At Troy, Grandma, and Momma's graves, I said prayers. I still missed my brother. So many memories, but over time, the pain of loss was replaced with the remembrance of love.

I drove by the old home place. There wasn't much left. The house I grew up in was gone. A pasture remained. New Site was about the same. People around here still farmed the land. There was only one gas station and a stop sign.

I stopped outside the New Site high school gym. They had a new one. It was about the only thing that had changed.

Standing there, memories reemerge of the gym where I played: sounds of balls clanking the rim while shooting around and being dribbled across the court, the smell of sweat, and the voice of Coach echoing in the gymnasium.

Coach Carver with his Styrofoam coffee cup in hand.

I smiled at the remembrance. Over fifty years have passed since that time I played for Coach.

A lifetime ago.

My lifetime.

I thought I was done, but I realized I still had one more place to go. I knew where the cemetery was. I had visited Coach's grave once or twice before. This time, though, I seemed to be drawn to it.

A heart attack took Coach Carver almost thirty years ago.

The news devastated me. The man meant a lot to me. I don't think I realized how much until he was gone.

Whenever I have struggled to believe in something, basketball had been there for me. My world collapsed, and basketball had gotten me through.

Coach Carver had gotten me through.

I wonder where I would be now if he hadn't shown up that night when I had been drinking. I know with certainty that my life would not have turned out the way it did if he hadn't cared.

Coach wanted not only me but all of us to succeed. He was there to help us when we needed it and pushed us when we wanted to quit.

When I went out into the world, he was the measuring stick by which I judged other men, only to discover that few measured up. He was a rare individual.

At times, I wonder if Coach Carver would have adjusted to this new brand of ball with the shot clock and three-point shots. Something tells me that he would have. He was the smartest coach I have ever been around. He could look into your eyes, and it was like he saw into your soul and saw what made you tick.

Coach taught me that nothing good comes easy. I have used that philosophy most of my life. When things were at their worst, I never gave up. Never. I have worked hard for everything I've gotten.

When I'm gone, I want my children and grandchildren to look back on my life and know I have no regrets. Life isn't perfect, but I've had a good life.

Crossing the cemetery, I walk over to Coach's grave and say a prayer.

My life was changed forever because of Coach Carver.

I am a better man because of him.

Lost in my thoughts, I look up to see the sun fade over the horizon. I hadn't realized how much time had passed since I stepped back into my past. I have to go. Debby will be expecting me.

Taking a deep breath, I soak in a feeling of deep peace. I turn to walk back to the car and feel my spirits lift as a sudden realization sweeps through me—the measure of a man isn't about awards or accolades. It's not money or possessions. The true measure of a man is the legacy he leaves behind.

The End

The Real Story of Behind The Measure of a Man

Coach Gerald Caveness demanded and received so much from his players. He had the ability to not only make believers out of his players, but he did something that most coaches couldn't or wouldn't do. He made believers in the community during an era when high school sports played a bigger role. Coach Caveness was an overachiever.

Coach Kermit Davis, former coach of Tupelo High School and Mississippi State University

March 8, 1969 saw the New Site Royals beat the Jackson Wingfield's Falcons, 72-70. This marked the first time a school other than an AA school won the overall title since the start of the new classifications. The Grand Slam was abolished in 1982 when it was deemed unfair to the lower classifications. For a short time, the tournament between State champions was brought back, but once again, it was halted.

Nestled in the heart of what was known as *Basketball Country*, New Site had an enrollment of a hundred and twenty-four students with the lowest classification due to size of B in 1969. From 1965-1969, the Royals won an unprecedented five consecutive State B championships. It was a far cry from when their coach first came to New Site.

Coach Gerald Caveness began coaching the Royals in 1960-61 season. The two prior years, the Royals had only won three games. Coach Caveness took the program and established a dynasty over the next nine years.

Gerald Caveness had been a great basketball player himself. He grew up on a farm not far from New Site in the rural community known as Marietta. His senior year, his high school team won the State B-BB championship. The All-State player was the captain of the team and leading scorer. From there he played at Northeast Mississippi Junior College, and Mississippi State University, where he twice made All-Southeastern Conference (SEC). After graduation he joined the Marines. There he played on the Marine team where he made All-Marine Corps team, the East Coast All-Star team, and played in the Service Olympic tryout. He was a phenomenal shooter known for being a marksman and a ball hawking ability.

Returning to Mississippi, Coach Caveness began his successful coaching career in Corinth and then went to Laurel. He came home to coach at New Site for nine years. After winning the Grand Slam, he retired from coaching for two years. He returned to coach at Booneville for eight years and then finished his career with eight years at Alcorn Central. There would be no more state championships despite coming close several times.

Twenty-nine years of coaching brought Coach Caveness many honors. Among them include Mississippi All Star Coach 1965, Mississippi Coach of the Year 1977, Region V Coach of the Year 1977, Region Coach of the Year 1987, and Mississippi Coaches Hall of Fame. Coach Caveness won 80% of his games with 657 wins and 181 losses. More amazing is the fact he never had a losing season.

At New Site, the Royals hold records that may never be broken. Starting in 1965, the New Site Royals won an astounding five consecutive State championships. During that run, the Royals won 45 straight District, North Half, and State tournament games. In this five-year period, the New Site teams won 92% of their games against the best teams in the state. Also, three seniors on the 1969 championship team hold the record of being the only ones to have played and won four consecutive State titles: David Denson, Tommy Brewer, and Jerry Harris.

Coach Caveness was renowned for developing players. He invented a patented device called the Sharpshooter to help with a player's shot. He believed in a disciplined team and had an innate ability to motivate players. One of his secrets on being successful—he was always prepared. He studied the game and knew the rulebook backward and forward.

This remarkable run was accomplished not only by a great coach, but great players and a wonderful community who supported their basketball program. These players and managers bought into what Coach Caveness told them from the beginning. The community came together.

Within New Site, a spirit was born that carried through Coach Caveness' tenure. A belief developed that all things were possible. Moreover, a pride was established of who they were and where they lived. A dream drove these kids onward. Coach Caveness brought them together to accomplish the impossible.

There is a need to preserve history. On this feat, Northeast Mississippi can take pride in their accomplishments.

Prentiss County was renowned for its basketball. It holds 32 State titles: Wheeler (11), Baldwyn (7), New Site (7), Booneville (4), Jumpertown (1), and Marietta (1). Prentiss County doesn't have any school in the largest division. Thirty minutes away from Prentiss County was Tupelo High School in Lee County, which won the Grand Slam three out of five years during this time (1965-69).

1965 Champions
Kneeling – L-R: Merle Shelton – Manager, Coach Gerald Caveness, James Beard – Manager
Standing – L-R: Ronnie White, Charles Jacobs, Truman Caviness, Terry Moore, Vernie Crowe, Wade Wilson, Larry Johnson
Gerald Cleveland, Sonny Shockley, Freddie Turvaville, James Downs

1965 New Site Royals

Ronnie White
Charles Jacobs
Truman Caviness
Terry Moore
Vernie Crowe
Wade Wilson
Larry Johnson
Gerald Cleveland
Fletcher (Sonny) Shockley
Freddy Turvaville
James Downs
Managers: Merle Shelton
              James Beard

1966 Champions

Front Row – L-R: Ronnie White, James Downs, David Denson, Jim Jacobs, Sonny Shockley, Jerry Harris, Larry Lambert – Manager, Jackie Woodruff – Manager

Back Row – L-R: Charles Jacobs, Tommy Brewer, Larry Johnson, Vernie Crowe, Wade Wilson, Herchell Barron, Coach Gerald Caveness

1966 New Site Royals

Charles Jacobs
Hershel Barron
Steve Johnson
Ronnie White
James Downs
David Denson
Jim Jacobs
Tommy Brewer
Larry Johnson
Vernie Crowe
Wade Wilson
Jerry Harris
Sonny Shockly
Managers: Larry Lambert
                Jackie Woodruff

1967 Champions
Kneeling – L-R: Larry Lambert - Manager, Jackie Woodruff - Manager,
Standing – L-R: James Downs, Ronnie White, Rex Berryman, Jim Jacobs, Charles Jacobs, Tommy Brewer, Coach Gerald Caveness,
Larry Gann, Larry Johnson, Jerry Harris, David Denson, Steve Johnson, Stan Riddle

1967 New Site Royals

James Downs
Larry Johnson
Rex Berryman
Tommy Brewer
Charles Jacob
Steve Johnson
Ronnie White
David Denson
Jerry Harris
Larry Gann
Stan Riddle
Jim Jacobs
Managers: Jackie Woodruff
            Larry Lambert

1968 Champions
Kneeling – L-R: Jackie Woodruff – Manager, Coach Gerald Caveness, Freddie Harris – Manager
Standing – L-R: Steve Johnson, Rex Berryman, Jim Jacobs, Jerry Harris, Terry Stockton, Larry Gann, Tommy Brewer, David Denson, Garry Kennedy, Stan Riddle

1968 New Site Royals

Rex Berryman
Steve Johnson
Tommy Brewer
David Denson
Jerry Harris
Stan Riddle
Larry Gann
Jim Jacobs
Terry Stockton
Gary Kennedy

Managers: Jackie Woodruff
             Freddie Harris

1969 Champions

Kneeling Front: Coach Gerald Caveness
Standing - L-R: Stan Riddle, Garry Kennedy, David Denson, Jim Jacobs, Sammy Tolar, Terry Stockton, Larry Gann, Tommy Brewer, Jerry Harris, Jerry Gann, Nicky Johnston, Gerald Jacobs

1969 New Site Royals

Jerry Harris
Tommy Brewer
David Denson
Larry Gann
Stan Riddle
Garry Kennedy
Terry Stockton
Jerry Gann
Sammy Tolar
Gerald Jacobs
Nicky Johnston
Jim Jacobs
Managers: Ricky Eaton
               Charles Davis
Assistant Coach: Randle Downs

Grand Slam 1969

1st Row – L-R: Freddy Harris, David Denson, Charles Davis, Larry Gann
2nd Row - L-R: James Melvin, Randle Downs, Terry Stockton, Coach Gerald Caveness, James Sparks, Ricky Eaton, Gerald Jacobs
3rd Row – L-R: Jerry Harris, Tommy Brewer, Stan Riddle, Nicky Johnston, Jerry Gann, Sammy Tolar, Garry Kennedy

Interesting True Tid-bits

In 1968, Coach Caveness and the New Site Royals went into the Grand Slam finals confident in his team abilities against Tupelo. The Royals had destroyed them on their only meeting of the year. The difference was Tupelo had gained a player by the name of Frank Dowsing. Frank Dowsing became the first black football player for Mississippi State. During my research, I discovered that Frank Dowsing was an amazing man in his own right. He was a phenomenal athlete who set a state record for the 100-yard dash. He earned all-conference honors in football, basketball, and track. At Mississippi State, Dowsing was named to All-America honors as a defensive back, Academic All-America team, and was voted Mr. Mississippi State. He was drafted by the Philadelphia Eagles and attended medical school. Mr. Dowsing opened the way for black integration into sports in the state.

As a high school player, Coach Gerald Caveness was on the 1950 State B-BB championship team at Marietta. I believe I would be remiss if I left out their accomplishment. His coach, Lyle Bullard, had a strong influence on Coach Caveness. Marietta was the only school I know that could have had a smaller enrollment than New Site. The Marietta Raiders were known as the Dream Team. Leading scorer and captain, Gerald Caveness earned All-State honors along with Clyde Jones and Gene Champion. Coach Bullard was quoted as saying, "This group of boys was an all-around team with plenty of ability, cooperation, and good sportsmanship. They have to be the greatest bunch of boys anywhere." They ended the season with a 45-1 record. Their lone loss during the regular season came to

Booneville, who won the A-AA State championship that year. (Marietta did beat Booneville during the regular season that year as well.)

All-state picks on the Marietta team are shown in the photo at top left with their coach, Lyle Bullard. Pictured left to right are Coach Bullard, Gene Champion, Gerald Caveness and Clyde Jones. These lads were chosen during the tournament at Jackson last week in which the Marietta team walked away with the State B-BB championship.

Coach Caveness' roommate while in the Marine Corps was Vince Dooley, who became the head coach for the University Georgia Bulldogs football team.

Dean and Troy Barnes are truly fictional characters. Both characters are a combination of players that Coach Caveness coached. All of his players influenced characters in the book and resemblances may be seen.

Truman Caviness who was on the 1965 B State championship team at New Site died in a car accident shortly after graduating from high school.

Personal Thoughts

In the folklore of early North Mississippi basketball, there are many miraculous stories as well as great players and amazing coaches. Coaches whose names and accomplishments will never be forgotten, such as Coach Bonner Arnold, Coach Harvey Childers, Coach Sam Richie, Coach Milton and Malcolm Kuykendall, Coach Larry McKay, Coach Jim Horton, Coach Kermit Davis, and Coach Ken Lindsey. Yet, there is one that left a unique set of fingerprints on basketball history— Coach Gerald Caveness. Coach Caveness was part of a remarkable story of not just championship teams with unbelievable achievements, but a coming together of a community for a single purpose. This fantastic basketball story is the Mississippi version of Hoosier's!!!
The story told here is much more than a tale of an incredible Coach. It's about a team and a rural community that believed and accomplished the improbable against all odds…And I was an eyewitness to these amazing events for he was my father.
Gary Caveness, son, former player

It was a privilege to get to play basketball for Coach Caveness whom I think was the best high school coach to ever coach the game. And, also, a very special person.
Terry Moore, former player

I'm glad to have gotten to play for Coach Caveness. I thought the world of him.
David Denson, former player

More than a coach.
Tommy Brewer, former player

Coach Caveness taught me discipline and to never give up. He used to say a 100 percent is not good enough. You have to give a 110 percent. You have to give it your all. Hard work pays off.
Jerry Harris, former player

Coach Caveness was way ahead of his time. I don't know anyone that played for him that didn't love him. He always said that anything worth doing, is worth doing right.
Larry Johnson, former player

In the last few years of his life, I was privileged to spend a lot of time with my father. During on of those times, he asked me, "Do you know why I was so hard on my players?"
I answered, "Because you wanted to win."
"Yes, I wanted to win," he said. "But more importantly, it was to help make them better men."
Not only did my father encourage his players to win at the game of basketball, but he also wanted them to win at life. He instilled the same in me. I'm proud to have called him Dad.
Greg Caveness, son, former player

Coach's ability of taking ten to twelve average players who were willing to learn, put in the work and develop them into a TEAM was phenomenal. The long hours of preparation weren't always fun, but the reward came on game day. Those years under his leadership are some of the most memorable times in my life. His encouragement and support inspired me to be the best player and teammate that I could be. He taught me so many lessons that have carried me far beyond the basketball court that still apply today.
Mitch Johnson, former player

Coach Caveness made a great impression on me. He knew the game better than anyone and knew how to get the maximum out of a kid.
Coach Milton Kuykendall

Coach Caveness was a great tactician and the best prepared coach I have ever been around. He could sell the kids an idea and make them believe they could do anything. Great coach.
Coach Malcom Kuykendall

I learned more basketball in my first year as Coach Caveness assistant than I learned in the many years of playing in high school and college.
Nelson Hight, former coach

Acknowledgements

I could not have written this book without a great deal of help. I want to thank everyone that shared their stories with me which include Terry Moore, David Denson, Tommy Brewer, Jerry Harris, Helen Harris, Larry Johnson, Mitch Johnson, Coach Kuykendall and Coach Kermit Davis.

I need to acknowledge that none of this would have been possible without the help and support of my brother, Gary Caveness.

I sincerely thank everyone I reached out to and willing gave me their time.

My sincere wish in writing this story was to reflect the spirit of the community that is New Site and Prentiss County.

If you want to catch my books when they are on special promotion and new releases,
Follow me on BookBub:

https://www.bookbub.com/authors/jerri-hines

https://www.bookbub.com/search?search=colleen+connally

Sign up for my newsletter:
http://madmimi.com/signups/226168/join

Books under Jerri Hines:

The Southern Legacy Series
Belle of Charleston
Shadows of Magnolia
Born to Be Brothers
The Sun Will Rise

Winds of Betrayal Series:
Winds of Betrayal
The Darkness of Deception
The Heavens Shall Fall
Set Fire To The Rain

WINDS OF CHANGE
The Governor's Daughter
The Bastard Son

The Measure of a Man – Standalone Coming of Age Novel

Books Under Penname Colleen Connally

Secret Lives Series:

Seductive Secrets
Broken Legacy
Seductive Lies

Boston's Crimes of Passion
Fragmented
Framed

Boston's Crimes of Horror
Scream for the Camera

The Three Realms
Past of Shadows
The Path Now Turned
Vision of Destiny